DEFYING THE EARL

LORDS IN LOVE #4

ERICA RIDLEY

ALSO BY ERICA RIDLEY

The *Dukes of War*:
The Viscount's Tempting Minx
The Earl's Defiant Wallflower
The Captain's Bluestocking Mistress
The Major's Faux Fiancée
The Brigadier's Runaway Bride
The Pirate's Tempting Stowaway
The Duke's Accidental Wife
A Match, Unmasked
All I Want

The *Wild Wynchesters*:
The Governess Gambit
The Duke Heist
The Perks of Loving a Wallflower
Nobody's Princess
My Rogue to Ruin

***Heist Club*:**
The Rake Mistake
The Modiste Mishap

***Rogues to Riches*:**
Lord of Chance
Lord of Pleasure
Lord of Night
Lord of Temptation

Lord of Secrets
Lord of Vice
Lord of the Masquerade

The *12 Dukes of Christmas*:
Once Upon a Duke
Kiss of a Duke
Wish Upon a Duke
Never Say Duke
Dukes, Actually
The Duke's Bride
The Duke's Embrace
The Duke's Desire
Dawn With a Duke
One Night With a Duke
Ten Days With a Duke
Forever Your Duke
Making Merry

***Gothic Love Stories*:**
Too Wicked to Kiss
Too Sinful to Deny
Too Tempting to Resist
Too Wanton to Wed
Too Brazen to Bite

***Magic & Mayhem*:**
Kissed by Magic
Must Love Magic
Smitten by Magic

Regency Fairy Tales

Bianca & the Huntsman

Her Princess at Midnight

Missing an Erica Ridley book?

Grab the latest edition of the free, downloadable and printable complete book list by series here:

https://ridley.vip/booklist

DEFYING THE EARL

LORDS IN LOVE #4

ACKNOWLEDGMENTS

As always, I could not have written this book without the invaluable support of many others. Huge thanks go out to Darcy Burke, Elyssa Patrick and Erica Monroe. You are the best!

I also want to thank my wonderful VIP readers, our Historical Romance Book Club on Facebook, and my fabulous early reader team. Your enthusiasm makes the romance happen.

Thank you so much!

CHAPTER 1

*T*itus Noble, the fifth Earl of Gilbourne, glared at the long queue of well-dressed revelers eager to enter the town of Marrywell's richly decorated assembly rooms.

He hated that he was one of the masses.

"Of all the ridiculous places to arrange a simple meeting..." he said under his breath as the crowd snaked closer to the open ballroom doors to the May Day fair welcome ball. The evening was dark and dreary, matching his disposition.

There was nothing convenient about this farce. His godmother, Lady Stapleton, had seen to that. She knew of Titus's disinclination to attend any event with young marriageable hopefuls—or, to be honest, any event that involved other people. Yet *where* did she arrange this damnable rendezvous?

The opening night gala of the annual Marrywell matchmaking festival, that's where.

"Five minutes," he muttered into the starched folds of his cravat. "I'll give it five minutes, and then I'm leaving."

Except he and his godmother both knew he'd stay

until he found her and picked up the infernal package, as requested.

Duty. His compulsive need to do the right thing drove his every action. He had never cursed it more.

After the death of his parents when Titus was twelve years old, he'd been remanded into his godparents' care. Fourteen years later, Titus's godfather was long gone, but Lady Stapleton was almost as spry —and certainly as scheming—as ever.

Apparently, she had a new ward to foster. One as willful and fractious as a mule. The recalcitrant chit had proved too much for the widow to manage. In hope that a firm hand would nudge her newly orphaned grand-niece onto a respectable path, Lady Stapleton was transferring control over to her godson.

Titus was the epitome of control. His unbreakable iron will was the one thing keeping him from roaring like a lion and charging back into his carriage as fleet as a cheetah.

Obviously he could keep a small slip of a girl in check. The problem was that he had no desire to do so. Titus lived alone for a reason.

A gaggle of debutantes bounded up to him like baby fawns approaching a bubbling stream. After extensive giggling amongst themselves, the bravest of the bunch stepped forward. She fluttered her eyelashes at Titus in faux flirtation, but her gaze slithered over his scars and failed to meet his eyes.

"My heavens, this queue is ever so long," she simpered, her voice falsetto. "Surely a lord such as yourself cannot object if we were to stand with you?"

Titus smote all six of them with his monstrous glare.

They blanched in unison and scurried off toward the end of the line, grasping at each other for strength and shooting fearful gazes over their pastel shoulders as they fled.

See? He would be a phenomenal guardian.

Even if every moment of it was against his will. Blast his godmother!

Everyone knew that the Earl of Gilbourne was an emotionless, rigid automaton who lived for pre-dictability and order. He was a dangerous beast who lived alone—save for his servants, who took care to stay out of his sight. Once this bothersome interlude ended, Titus intended to continue his self-isolation until the day he died.

Between his estates and the House of Lords, he had a surplus of responsibilities to keep him busy. There was no room in his exacting schedule for a frivolous soirée in some country village, just as there was no room in his quiet, peaceful, meticulously structured life for an unexpected ward.

At last, it was Titus's turn to enter the ballroom.

"Your calling card, my lord?" asked the nauseat-ingly cheerful footman stationed at the door. "Oh! You must be—"

"You will *not* announce my name to this crowd," Titus growled.

The footman wilted, then scrounged up a pan-icked smile. "Er... Do go in, my lord. Please, have a lovely night."

Titus glowered back and stormed inside.

He never smiled, and he never laughed, and he was not at all bothered by his lack of unnecessary fa-cial contortions. Life was neither funny nor fun. Why pretend to be enjoying it?

There was certainly nothing to look forward to in a circus like *this*.

He cast his dark gaze about the crowded ball-room, scanning for his godmother. With her snow white hair adorned with a trio of omnipresent ostrich feathers, she should be simple to spot, even in a beehive like this one.

There was no sign of Lady Stapleton anywhere.

No doubt fashionably late, just to make him suffer. Titus ground his teeth and stalked to a position against the wall opposite the main doors, so that he would be the first to see his godmother make her entrance.

If either woman thought for a second that he intended to stomach this matchmaking carnival for a single moment longer than absolutely necessary, they were about to discover how badly they had erred.

The moment she strode in the door, Titus would intercept her—and the package. A twenty-year-old unruly orphan by the name of Miss Dodd. At which point, Titus would summarily stuff said orphan into his carriage, and drive the hell out of Marrywell, even if they didn't arrive at his London town home until dawn.

The plan was simple: Get the ward, and get out.

That easy. Or it would be, if his ward and godmother showed. Titus clenched his jaw. For a man whose painstaking plans were legendary, it was absolutely galling for tonight's handoff not to be going according to plan.

Lady Stapleton and her ward were supposed to be here *first*.

Waiting for *him*.

He was supposed to swoop in and scoop up the ward, press a kiss to his godmother's cheek, and then exit these premises before anyone had a chance to recognize him. Never to be seen in rural Hampshire —or, indeed, outside of the capital's borders—again.

He hadn't planned for *this*.

"Oh, pardon me," said a well-coiffed young buck

with an affable smile. "The Earl of Gilbourne, I dare-say. Do you know where they've tucked the card room?"

Titus incinerated him with a glare.

The young buck slunk off like a kicked puppy with his tail between his legs.

A matchmaking fair was a mindbogglingly silly place to take possession of a ward. Titus chafed at being forced to mingle with other people. If the rumor got out that an unmarried earl walked amongst them… The onslaught of fluttering lashes and dropped handkerchiefs would be untenable. If indeed it was possible to keep his identity hidden. One look, and the astute would know.

They should also know that this reclusive earl wasn't interested in exchanging a single word with any of these teeming strangers. Much less stand up for a dance with some desperate debutante. No doubt Lady Stapleton knew exactly what she was about when she'd arranged for him to meet her here on this battleground. Although Titus had told her time and again that the title would die with him, she insisted it was just a matter of meeting the right person.

Titus hated meeting *anyone*. The last thing a man like him needed… was…

All coherent thought fled from his brain.

There, cutting across the ballroom floor as if absolutely oblivious to the hundreds of whirling couples waltzing in time around her, was the most beautiful woman Titus had ever seen.

Thick, chestnut hair with just a hint of red. A flawless oval face with flushed pink cheeks and plump lips the color of a ripe pomegranate. Not too slender or too round but right in the middle, with an abundance of soft curves. Tall for a woman, though

9

she would barely crest Titus's shoulder in height. Eyes the color of... He couldn't quite tell from this distance.

He found himself tracking her every move, in the hopes she might glance in his direction and allow him to solve the mystery of the hue of her irises.

Titus willed his boots to stay rooted into the ground, but found himself taking a step closer.

She'd crossed the ballroom and was now on *Titus's* side of the room. The refreshment tables were here as well, sandwiched between awkward rows of presumably decorative potted ferns that could double as privacy screens.

Was that what she wanted? Privacy? Titus empathized viscerally with the desire to suck in a restorative breath of sweet solitude to escape this crowd, before stepping out from behind a folding screen—or a wall of potted plants, as it were. The thick fronds partially obscured her from view. He couldn't tear his gaze away.

Her thick waves of red-brown hair looked so touchably soft. As did her smooth ivory skin and, well, everything else about her. To look at her was to yearn to pull her close, to draw her into his hungry embrace and never let her go.

Which meant the *last* thing a creature like Titus ought to do was edge closer.

And yet...

He tried to shake this strange stupefaction from his spinning head. He and the mystery woman hadn't been formally introduced, which meant he was not to approach her under any circumstances. Nor did she appear to have a nearby companion, chaperone, or relative from whom he could beg an introduction— not that he *would*.

To do so would be to imply interest, and Titus was militantly careful never to show interest.

Even in someone who looked this sweet and lost and kissable.

He swallowed hard. Thank the lord above his godmother had not yet arrived. If she caught the tiniest whiff of temporary infatuation, she'd pull a parson out of her bonnet and have the wedding rites read here and now.

Lady Stapleton had tried everything in her power to convince Titus to marry. The last remaining straw to grasp was his commitment to duty. *Lords must beget heirs* was a primary mandate, and the reason a good number of those in this ballroom were present tonight.

It was also the one and only rule Titus unapologetically ignored.

The rest of the beau monde's absurd codes of conduct? Not a problem. Titus *adored* rules. The more the merrier. Rules made the world go 'round. Rules were the track at the hippodrome, and the crack of the starting pistol. How else would you win the race if you didn't know when and where to run?

Titus *excelled* at rules. He was unparalleled in creating them, adhering to them, enforcing them. Yes, he refused to be a husband or a father, but he was otherwise a perfect *earl*. And as such, he needn't explain his motives or reasons to anyone.

Including his meddling godmother.

Reminded of her absence, Titus sent a halfhearted glance about the brimming ballroom before returning his focus to the young lady standing between the refreshment table and the closest row of potted plants.

Her gaze was on the swarming dance floor, not on Titus, which was why he still could not discern the color of her eyes—despite apparently having taken several more involuntary steps in her direction.

His unusual behavior was rash and nonsensical. Or on the contrary, perhaps simple enough to explain: he was a man consumed by loneliness. A motivator even stronger than duty, and the real reason he threw himself wholeheartedly into the House of Lords. A busy man did not have *time* to be lonely.

A constant personal refrain he would never admit, even under pain of death.

Why should he? Titus didn't *need* anyone. Which was a good thing, since he didn't *have* anyone. Solitary was better. Solitary was simple. Solitary was safest for everyone.

But his gaze flicked back toward the young woman, who was still standing—inconceivably —alone.

All right, he would give it fifteen minutes. If his godmother arrived within the next quarter hour, Titus would forget the beautiful young lady, deal with his business, and go directly home.

But if a quarter hour passed and his godmother still hadn't arrived...

Titus might saunter just close enough to make out the color of the young woman's eyes and put paid to the mystery. The solution to an idle riddle. Nothing more and nothing less.

And if the young lady chanced to meet his gaze... If, god forbid, she *spoke* to him... What would happen then?

For once, Titus had no idea. Thank heavens she had not yet spied him watching her. For the first time in decades, the Earl of Gilbourne found himself without a comprehensive plan.

He'd just have to see what happened next.

CHAPTER 2

*M*iss Matilda Dodd hovered between a towering pile of cakes and an even taller row of dense potted ferns. From this position, she was perfectly visible—if you happened to be at the refreshment table or on the dance floor. Her great-aunt was at neither of these locales, making it the perfect place to hide in plain sight.

Moments earlier, they had entered the retiring room side by side. But as soon as Aunt Stapleton ducked behind the first folding screen, Matilda disappeared from the retiring room altogether.

Who could blame her? Matilda had lived her entire life in a hamlet even smaller than Marrywell, which was, at first glance, a charming town positively overrun with fashionable lords and ladies. Or at least, merrymakers significantly more fashionable than Matilda herself.

At this unwelcome reminder of her humble appearance, she dipped her fingers into her previously overstuffed reticule, withdrew yet another tiny square of candied fruit peel, and popped it into her mouth. *Lemon.* Delicious. Who could feel overwhelmed and panicked with the sensation of sweet citrus exploding in her mouth?

Fortunately, Matilda *wanted* this experience. She had never been to a ball in all her life, and now that she was here, she wanted to enjoy it. Was that too much to ask?

Apparently yes, if your name was the Earl of Gilbourne. Matilda's unwanted new guardian. Oh, she was sure he was a perfectly fine man. According to Aunt Stapleton, her godson was "regal" and "reserved", which Matilda interpreted as *handsome* and *shy*.

Shyness was something Matilda deeply understood, and was actively trying to change about herself. It wasn't that she didn't like people. She adored crowds, and yearned to be the life of the party. Matilda just didn't know *how*; what to do, what to say. Until today, she'd never had the opportunity to learn, or even to try.

According to Aunt Stapleton, the singular opportunity might not repeat itself. Aunt had arranged the transfer here, so that Matilda could at least *glimpse* what an active social life might be like, but she'd warned her that the reclusive earl would whisk her away the moment Matilda was in his clutches. He'd never step foot outside his London town home again.

After almost twenty years of provincial boredom, followed by an even darker year of heartbroken mourning, the last thing Matilda wanted was to lock herself back inside a bedchamber and stare at the ceiling in loneliness all day.

The earl would no doubt be able to forcibly remove her from this assembly room once Aunt presented him to his new ward. Which gave Matilda no choice but to evade them both, and drink in this colorful new environment whilst she still could.

In short, she was blatantly eavesdropping.

"Was that the Duke of Southbury in the garden?" whispered one debutante to another as she piled a plate with cakes.

"Of course not," said her companion. "The Duke of Southbury is not looking for a bride, and if he were, he would do so at Almack's, not here."

A thrill rushed through Matilda. She'd learnt so much in her first few minutes. She could name half a dozen members of the ton, most of whom were here tonight. She'd seen the May Queen, who would be selecting seven maidens fair during some sort of crowning ceremony. She'd glimpsed Mr. Radford, the man who owned the botanical gardens, speaking to the woman in charge of the cakes.

And she'd learned she herself was functionally invisible, despite standing within arm's reach of the plates.

Doubt and embarrassment warred within her. Matilda stood taller. Her objective in life was to have a grand adventure. But her greatest fear was that she was too insignificant for even a tiny one.

Aunt Stapleton had made a point of explaining that this festival catered to people of all walks of life, from the haut ton to the local farmers. And yet, Matilda still received less notice than a fly upon the wall.

Which only made her reconnaissance all the more important. She was determined to make these people like her—even if most would not fully accept her. The only way to succeed was to first figure out just what she was up against. She soaked in every overheard snippet like a sponge. If someone asked her where to find the follies or the Cork & Cupid tavern, she could answer perfectly, despite never having clapped eyes on either sight. She knew the flavor of

15

every available cake, could name the songs in every upcoming set, and had learnt the Marquess of Creslow had contracted the services of a matchmaker.

All she needed was for someone to *ask* her something. It needn't be one of the details she'd overheard. She'd be happy to provide her name, for example. Or exchange a simple, "How do you do?"

If her shy guardian succeeded in shuttering Matilda away, she'd lose any chance for adventure. This could be her one and only opportunity to mingle with society. Here. Now.

She straightened her shoulders and pasted on a welcoming smile, hoping against hope that someone —anyone—should ask her to dance, even if doing so would quickly give her position away. The experience would be worth it.

Besides, Aunt Stapleton wouldn't cause a stir until after the set ended. Matilda would at least have one memory of how it felt to dance before an orchestra. And in a fashionable crush, like this one!

But so far, it wasn't as simple as turning up and accepting a dance. No one offered her so much as a polite greeting. At this point, she'd gratefully accept a smile—or even a fleeting glance.

Country life had been simple. Losing her parents and surviving the subsequent year of mourning had been terrible. This was something else entirely. Matilda had never expected to be a debutante. She was too old, for one. Most of these young women would've been "out" for three or four seasons by the time they were on the cusp of turning twenty-one.

It wasn't just that Matilda didn't fit in. No one wanted her to. No one wanted *her*.

Or so they thought.

If her brush with death and the loss of her family

16

had taught her anything, it was that life was a gift that could disappear at any moment. The best anyone could do was make as much as possible of the days God granted them. Matilda intended to befriend the whole world by sheer force of will.

She popped another piece of candied peel into her mouth. *Orange.* Delightful. Everything seemed possible, no matter how unlikely, when one sucked upon a delicious piece of—

She felt the weight of his gaze before she saw him. It wrapped around her like a warm blanket on a... well, on an already humid and stuffy night. She didn't need to be warmed up. She needed adventure.

And the stranger's heated gaze felt like it might be a good one.

Slowly, Matilda cast her own gaze about as subtly as she could until she found the source of the shiver-inducing sensation. It didn't take long. He was two arm-lengths away, on the opposite side of the row of potted ferns. Watching her from their shadows, rather than from the brightly lit dance floor.

Or perhaps he preferred shadows. Despite the patchwork of scars covering half of his face, he was breathtakingly handsome. In a hulking, razor-sharp, terrifying sort of way. A beast amongst sheep.

She liked his mystique. She already liked *him*.

Adventure? He was the very definition.

"—with the Earl of Gilbourne?" said one debutante to another as they reached for a glass of lemonade.

Matilda gasped and stepped back against the shadowed wall herself, as if this stranger saying the name of her new guardian aloud should be enough to conjure him from the air. She wasn't ready to be whisked away. Not now, when things were starting to happen.

"Marry him?" The other debutante gave an exaggerated shudder. "He never smiles, he never laughs, and he looks like—"

The girls turned away from the table, and the orchestra swallowed up the rest of their gossip.

Heart pounding, Matilda kept her spine against the wall until her breath slowed. False alarm. She could not imagine being as famous as an earl. Gilbourne's name was on everyone's lips, and he wasn't even here.

Or was he? Was that why the debutantes had mentioned him?

Matilda scanned the ballroom for signs of her great-aunt. If the Earl of Gilbourne were here, Aunt Stapleton would be deep in conversation with him by now.

But there was no sign of her great-aunt. Perhaps she was still in the retiring room, waiting for her great-niece. Matilda tamped down a pang of guilt. She loved her great-aunt, and was resentful she was being passed along like outgrown rags. Especially if the gossips were right.

The Earl of Gilbourne never smiled, never laughed, and never left his home? What a prince. Matilda could already tell he would be a thorn in her side.

The gentleman watching her from the shadows of a potted fern, though... Now *he* was interesting.

She darted another glance in his direction. He hadn't exactly swept her off her feet—he hadn't even approached her yet, much less spoken to her—but every time he thought she wasn't looking, his dark gaze settled upon her once more.

Obviously *she* was the one who would need to take action.

She popped another small square of candied peel

into her mouth for strength. All right, three candied peels. Maybe five. She had no idea what she was doing, but she was determined to see it through. After all, she was less than a month shy of her majority. The day she turned one-and-twenty, she'd be able to live life on her own terms. As her new self: Miss Matilda Dodd, impossible-to-tie-down adventure-seeker. No one, not even her stuffy new guardian, would be able to hold her back.

She turned slightly. The terrifyingly handsome gentleman with the scarred face caught her looking.

He didn't look away.

Matilda gave him a fleeting, tentative smile.

His dark gaze only increased in intensity, scalding her with its heat until she was certain the diced peels in her reticule had melted into lemonade.

His skin was white, but his scars were whiter. A crisscross of raised webbing from his left temple to the base of his jaw. His hair was a dark brown, his eyes even darker. Almost black. The combination of light and dark was striking, but then, so was the rest of him. He was incredibly tall, and intimidatingly broad. A massive wall of a man, encased in buttery soft black superfine. A dazzlingly white cravat with knife-sharp folds fell from his chin to his chest.

And what a chest it was. Muscular and broad, tapering to a trim waist that led to equally powerful thighs.

Where Matilda was from, these were the muscles of someone who broke wild horses and rowed oars for hours. Was this man from the country, as well? Despite his brawn, he appeared much too fine to be the sort who sloshed through rivers and mucked out stalls. But muscles like that didn't form from lounging about gentlemen's clubs drinking port and playing whist.

ERICA RIDLEY

Without taking her eyes from his, she inched toward him until most of her body was hidden from the public behind the first of the potted ferns.

He did the same on his side, though the six-foot ferns barely reached his forehead.

Matilda gave him her most winning grin. "How do you do?"

"I'm still deciding." His voice was a deliciously low rumble. He looked as though he wanted to swallow her whole.

"I'm fine, thank you," she blurted out, although he had not asked. She rallied and tried again. "What's your name?"

"No." His tone was final.

She blinked. "Your name is… 'No'?"

"If you don't know it, I shan't give it. I don't want yours, either."

She swallowed. "Then what *do* you want?"

His stern lips tightened rather than respond, but his smoldering gaze held the answer. *Her.* He wanted Matilda.

A frisson of—awareness? danger? reckless abandon?—danced across her skin. This was much better than being some stodgy recluse's cloistered ward. Flirting wasn't nearly as difficult as she'd imagined. When Matilda married, it would be someone she chose on her own terms. Perhaps this gentleman right here.

Over his shoulder, a not-too-distant trio of ostrich feathers poked into the air. *Aunt Stapleton.* She was out of the retiring room and looking for Matilda. It wouldn't take her long to try the refreshment area.

With alacrity, Matilda hurried to hide herself deeper behind the ferns… and promptly tripped over her own feet.

In the space of a blink, the scarred stranger was

right there to save her. He caught her against his broad chest and wrapped his thick arms ever so gently about her.

"Thank you," she whispered.

He didn't answer. Or let her go.

"My hero," she added, and lifted her chin to kiss the cheek closest to her mouth.

He flinched and turned his head—either because he hadn't realized it was only a simple kiss, or because he didn't want her lips to touch his scars. But in turning his cheek away, he brought his mouth closer. Their lips touched.

At first, Matilda was too startled to pull away. When she finally regained some semblance of her wits, she was too *intrigued* to pull away. She'd never kissed a man before, and so far, she quite liked it. His lips were somehow both soft and firm. His embrace, strong and warm.

She knew he hadn't meant to kiss her. Any moment now, he would realize their mistake and push her away.

But if he did not... This could be the beginning of a wonderful new adventure.

CHAPTER 3

*T*itus froze in place, not quite able to credit the sudden series of unlikely events that had led to the unlikeliest event of all.

First: Titus Noble, the man who refused to exit the safety of his home except to fulfill his duty in the House of Lords, had driven eight hours to a provincial village in Hampshire.

Second: This same man, who had vowed to live and die alone, was at the Marrywell annual *matchmaking* festival, of all places, to take possession of an unwanted ward.

Third: And this same man, who wrapped himself in protective layers of propriety, save the occasional perfunctory encounter with a paid courtesan with the curtains drawn and the candles blown out, was standing behind a potted fern in an ornately lit public ballroom, with his arms around a total stranger, whose rose-petal lips still pressed sweetly to his own.

Titus had to put a stop to the madness before it consumed him. And yet, peeling this baffling woman's soft curves from the hard planes of his body did not appear to be a feat currently within his power to achieve.

It was the kiss's fault.

He hadn't meant to steal one. Or to have one stolen from *him*, as it were. Indeed, after the childhood accident, Titus had made it a lifelong practice not to allow his face within touching distance of anyone else's. Which made this the first time anyone, anywhere, had ever kissed him on the lips.

Six-and-twenty years old. His first kiss. And no doubt, his final one.

By God, he would make it count.

Rather than push the pretty stranger from his chest, he cradled her closer. Angled his head. Increased the pressure. Coaxed her into parting those perfect lips. Melted inside.

Heaven help him, she tasted like candied citrus. Orange and lemon and sweet sugar. It was not a flavor he'd been expecting. Yet now that he'd tasted it, he ardently believed all first kisses should taste exactly like this one.

Her arms wrapped about him tighter. It felt like… a hug. His mind swam with dizziness. No one had ever *held* him before, not since he was a small child. His limited encounters with courtesans had involved the least amount of preamble possible. No one else but his valet was ever permitted to touch him.

That this woman did not even know his name was the only reason he was allowing the kiss to continue at all. Well, that, and the fact that he enjoyed the feel of… everything about her. The softness of her body, the warmth of her curves, the eagerness of her mouth beneath his, the sugared spice of her kisses.

If they were anywhere else—and if Titus were *anyone* else—he would wish to continue kissing her indefinitely. Was tempted to do just that, here in this ballroom, behind a row of ferns that in no way provided the same privacy as a brick wall and a locked door.

It was the threat of someone else's gaze intruding, more than anything, that caused him to at last remove her from his arms and set her at a safe distance.

"That was very foolish," he told her repressively. Or perhaps he was reminding himself.

Her mouth looked plump and freshly kissed, and her warm brown eyes sparkled unrepentantly. "You stole the second kiss."

"You started it."

"You didn't stop me."

Yes. A fair point, one which he would examine in great detail later. In between reliving every moment of that extraordinary kiss.

"I'm putting a stop to it now," he said firmly. "This is a ballroom, not a—"

Blast. The floppy strands of a trio of bouncing ostrich feathers was approaching the row of potted plants. Somehow, his godmother had managed to sniff out Titus's concealed location, and was heading in this direction with his unwanted new ward in tow.

"Go back the way you came. *Hurry.*" He spun the pretty stranger back toward the refreshment table whilst he took a frantic step sideways out from the line of plants.

It was too late.

"There you are, Titus," said his beaming godmother, in a voice loud enough to carry all the way to London. "I see you've met your ward."

CHAPTER 4

$\mathcal{T}$itus stared at his godmother in horror. Then he stared at his—ward?—in horror. Then he closed his horrified eyes and lifted his grimacing face toward the heavens as if he could undo the last fifteen minutes of folly with the power of his will.

His ward's sweet-orange taste remained on his tongue.

"*This*," he growled dangerously as he opened his eyes to glare at his godmother, "is my ward?"

"Miss Matilda Dodd," Lady Stapleton confirmed cheerfully. "The orphaned young lady you promised to protect and to guide."

"I felt guided," chirped the ward, tossing him a saucy wink.

Titus ignored her. He narrowed his eyes at his godmother instead. "Where have you been this past quarter hour? She was supposed to be under your control."

"And I told you Matilda has proven singularly difficult to control. *You* said all she needed was a firm hand. Therefore, I leave you to it."

"Wait," he said desperately. "Don't go."

Lady Stapleton looked at him in amusement. *"I am not going anywhere. There's a tart-and-pie competition in the morning. You're the one who said you weren't staying."*

"I'm not staying," he echoed in relief, then cast a reproving glare at Miss Dodd. *"We're not staying."*

"I don't mind staying," she replied, as if he had posed a question rather than issue a decree. "I rather enjoy pies. Why don't I spend one more night with Aunt Stapleton? You and I can... *resume*... in the morning."

"No," he said coldly. "No pies, no Aunt Stapleton, and no resuming anything that has already happened. You're to comport yourself with complete decorum and propriety at all times whilst in my custody and under my protection."

Miss Dodd widened her eyes in faux innocence. "Complete decorum and propriety... like you have demonstrated?"

"Good heavens," said Lady Stapleton with a chuckle, "of course you wouldn't know, darling. The Earl of Gilbourne is synonymous with good ton. His unimpeachable comportment is part of why he's one of the most respected and influential members of the beau monde. If anyone can take you in hand and turn you into this year's diamond—"

"No," said Titus. "I cannot—*will* not—do it."

It wasn't just that he'd kissed the ward he'd promised to protect from nefarious advances. He was furious to discover she was the sort of girl who was out here kissing random strangers to begin with. He was not proud to count himself amongst her conquests.

"I understand the transition will take effort on both your parts," Lady Stapleton said gently. "Matilda has not been instructed in proper decorum the way young ladies of the ton have been molded all their lives. But you cannot hold her country upbringing against her."

The only thing Titus wanted to hold against her was—

He tamped down the thought. No. There would be no more kissing, and certainly no lusting. He had already done far too much. As for his ward...

If Miss Dodd weren't such a green bumpkin, she'd realize that she'd technically just been compromised by an earl. Husband-hunt over. Game won. Her ignorance was the only reason he'd emerged from the ferns unscathed and unbetrothed.

He might have dodged that bullet once, but he must take greater care from this moment onward. Titus needn't only shelter his ward from the ungentlemanly desires of others. He'd have to protect her from himself.

"Is it true he never laughs or smiles?" Miss Dodd stage-whispered to Lady Stapleton.

Titus's godmother sent an indulgent grin in his direction. "It's Gilbourne's sole character failing."

He glared at them both in response.

"Now, Titus," Lady Stapleton reprimanded him. "When you launch Matilda into society, she needs more than a wealthy, titled husband."

He stared at her. "What else can she want?"

"A love match," his godmother said firmly. "Perhaps you can finally find one for yourself, while you're at it."

Both he and his ward sent Lady Stapleton matching disgruntled expressions.

"I won't marry anyone he picks out," said Miss Dodd. "I'll select my own husband or take none at all, thank you very much."

"I am not now, nor will I ever be, in the market

for a wife," Titus reminded his godmother firmly. "Nor have I any wish to take part in the marriage mart, even second-hand. If you want Miss Dodd to parade about Almack's, you must take her there yourself."

Lady Stapleton sighed. "Would it kill you to attend a social event voluntarily for once in your life?"

He pointed at the scarred side of his face. "It might."

His godmother lowered her voice. "The chances of a tragedy like that striking again—"

"—are as high as they've ever been," he finished.

Crowds. Traffic. The deafening snap of an axle, followed by the sickening sway of an out-of-control carriage tipping over the side of a bridge and tumbling to the rocks below.

Accidents could happen to anyone. At any time.

It was why Titus would not be acquiring a wife or begetting children of his own. He'd already had everyone he'd ever loved ripped from him once. He refused to give Fate any opportunity to rob him of happiness and love all over again.

Solitude was better. Staying home was safe. Adding an impulsive ward into the mix...

"Miss Dodd is right," Titus said. "You should keep her with you. There's no reason I should be involved in any part of Miss Dodd's life or future."

"No reason? You're the Earl of Gilbourne, Titus. The very fact that you go nowhere and give no one your approval means that your chaperonage of Matilda will launch her into the highest echelons from the first moment you two enter a parlor."

"I am unqualified for—"

Lady Stapleton's palms flashed up in the air as if she'd just dropped a hot potato. "She's yours until she turns twenty-one. I'm an old lady, Titus. It's your turn now."

He gritted his teeth. "When does she turn twenty-one?"

"'She' is standing right here," said Miss Dodd. "I am age twenty and eleven months. My birthday is in three weeks."

Three weeks. Surely a man could survive three weeks of just about anything.

"And after that?" he asked.

"She comes into an inheritance," Lady Stapleton answered.

"I come into my *independence*," Miss Dodd corrected her. "Three weeks from now, I will not require the interference of Lord Gilbourne or any man. I shall be free to do as I please."

God save them all.

Obviously this chit could not be allowed to run wild. She'd attended her first ball for all of five minutes before she was kissing strangers behind a potted plant. Titus's original pronouncement was truer than he'd even realized: Miss Dodd was in want of a firm hand.

If he didn't want to be the guardian to provide it —and her great-aunt refused to take Miss Dodd back —then there was only one possible solution.

He must marry this chit off to the first fool willing to take her off his hands.

How difficult could it be?

CHAPTER 5

*M*atilda could not believe that the angry
lord scowling at her so thunderously
was the same gentleman who had kissed her senseless not ten minutes prior.

Now that she was seeing him in the bright light of
a thousand candles instead of the shadows behind a
row of ferns, he looked... Even more like the path to
adventure than ever. *Regal*, her great-aunt had said.
Matilda supposed so. The earl acted like a king and
held himself like a god. No doubt he was used to
people falling at his feet in supplication at the merest
glance of those intense, so-dark-gray-they're-almost-
black eyes.

Eyes that were busy glittering at her in open dis-
approval.

As if she had done all the kissing on her own! All
right, yes, she had *started* the kissing all on her own.
And it was becoming mortifyingly obvious that there
should never have been any kissing at all, if she had
not taken it upon herself to lift her lips toward his
cheek.

But after that! There had definitely been an after!
One in which he had engaged his mouth and tongue

every bit as willingly as she had, no matter how much he now regretted his complicit participation.

To think, she had actually for a moment believed she'd found a man she might wish to marry! Matilda scoffed at her own foolish naivety. This earned herself a deepened scowl from the earl and a confused look from her great-aunt, who had blessedly failed to witness just what her godson and great-niece had been doing behind those ferns.

And now this big illogical ox intended to marry her off to someone else?

Matilda scoffed again. Louder and scoffier. Ha! Double ha! If this encounter had taught her anything, it was that she shouldn't give the slightest encouragement to any priggish stick-in-the-mud suitor whom the Earl of Gilbourne determined possessed a "firm hand" capable of keeping Matilda in check.

She had no interest in being controlled, or reined in, or even citified. She would meet the right man on her own, and in good time. If it took years, so be it. She was twenty-one days away from a small fortune and complete independence. She would soon be having far too much *fun* with her newfound freedom to give two figs about the shocked sensibilities of know-all men like the Earl of Gilbourne.

He wrapped his enormous hand about her upper arm.

She glared at him.

"Come," he ordered, as if she were his trained pet. "We're leaving."

Matilda wanted to do nothing more than dig the heels of her dancing slippers into the parquet and stand her ground, but such a tantrum would do little to convince him that she was not a child in need of a nanny.

In desperation, she sent a beseeching look at her great-aunt. "Please. I want to stay."

"You're not my ward anymore," replied Aunt Stapleton gently. "What happens next is up to you and Lord Gilbourne."

Which meant, up to Lord Gilbourne, period. He clearly had no intention of inquiring after Matilda's desires, much less catering to them.

"We're leaving," he said sternly.

His fingers tightened around her arm. Not hard enough to bruise, or even to cause discomfort. Just enough pressure to convey *I am in charge and you are not.*

"We'll see about that," Matilda muttered beneath her breath.

She allowed him to steer her from the ballroom, but sent him no shortage of icy glares, so that he would know exactly how she felt about his unsympathetic high-handedness.

Her frostiest glares did not seem to bother him in the slightest.

The moment the trio stepped foot out-of-doors, the earl barked, "*My carriage.*" at a boy half Matilda's age.

"How's he supposed to know which—" she began.

The lad took off running. Seconds later, the sound of horse hoofs rose in the air. A stately coach-and-four driven by a man old enough to be Matilda's father pulled into view.

The driver tipped his hat at Matilda. "Your trunk is in the carriage, madam."

She stared at him. "But I left all of my... How did you..."

"Well, then," said Aunt Stapleton briskly. "It looks as though Titus has the situation under control. He's a good man, Matilda. You'll have a lovely time... or at least a new experience. Try to enjoy your evening. I'll be returning home to Shropshire myself after the tart-and-pie competition tomorrow."

With that, Aunt Stapleton gave each of them a kiss on their cheeks and disappeared back inside the crowded assembly rooms to enjoy the music and the dancing, without an apparent care in the world.

Matilda stared after her in disbelief.

"Get into the carriage," the earl growled in her ear.

She turned to chide him for being so demanding, only to see that the driver was indeed standing at the ready, one hand holding open the door whilst the other arm clutched his hat to his chest as he bent in a bow.

Cheeks heating in embarrassment, she hurried forward and allowed the driver to hand her inside. Lord Gilbourne climbed in after her and scowled when he saw where she had seated herself.

"I must take the rear-facing seat, mustn't I?" she blurted self-consciously. "I'm the one of lower rank."

"Sit on the forward-facing seat," he ordered.

"But you're an earl—"

"And you're a woman."

"But you're older—"

"By five years, not five decades."

"But Aunt Stapleton said I must make an attempt at 'town polish' for your sake—"

He slid his hands beneath her arms and moved her bodily from one padded bench to the other, depositing her on the good seat like a sack of potatoes. "Mayhap now we can both agree that my godmother does not know what is best for everyone."

A beat passed in silence.

"How long is the drive to London?" she asked in a small voice.

"Eight hours."

"Then at least *share* the best seat with me." She scooted toward the window and indicated the vast amount of available space by her side. The wide bench could easily accommodate *three* earls beside her. Well, two of his stature.

With an aggrieved expression, Lord Gilbourne moved her to the opposite side of the bench and arranged himself on the seat next to her so that she was facing the unscarred half of his face.

Matilda immediately altered her previous calculations. The bench only fit *one* Earl of Gilbourne. His outsized presence seemed to take up the entire carriage, from carpet to ceiling. He was certainly consuming all of the available oxygen. Her lungs could barely manage to remember to breathe.

This is all part of the adventure, she told herself firmly. *An amusing anecdote you will one day tell to your grandchildren.*

She might not tell them how good Lord Gilbourne smelled, though. Soap and bergamot and spice. Or how broad his shoulders were, and how entranced she was by the improbable girth of his muscles.

But she'd tell them he was impossible.

"You can smile if you want to," she told him. "You won. I'm in the carriage. And no one is here to see you gloat."

He sent her a look so scathing, it was a wonder every hair on her body didn't burn to a crisp.

No smiles, then. Even in private.

Pity.

Matilda hated that she found him every bit as attractive when he was cold and angry as she did when he was hot and kissing her.

The earl leaned forward to tap the driver's panel,

to indicate that they were ready. The horses glided into motion at once. Matilda had never been in a carriage this smooth. It was nothing like bumping along in a dog cart. More like floating on a sturdy raft down a peaceful river.

Lord Gilbourne looked as though he'd never been less comfortable in his life.

"How many hours did you say?" she asked tentatively.

He sent her a look. "Eight."

"And it's already eight o'clock at night?"

"Eight forty-five."

This was pronounced without a visible glance at a pocket watch, yet Matilda had no doubt that Lord Gilbourne was right. He was the sort of man who was always right. Who expected reality itself to heed his commands—and often got what he wished for.

"You don't think... you might be more comfortable spending the night in a bed, rather than a carriage, and traveling home in the daylight tomorrow when we can see the countryside through the windows?"

His gaze shot up to the driver's panel, then back to her. His jaw worked in silence for a moment, then he leaned forward and slid open the panel. "John Coachman! Blushing Maid Inn, please."

"You have lodgings booked for tonight?" she asked.

"I have lodgings rented for all week," he answered dryly. "Courtesy of your great-aunt, who arranged this travesty."

"You have an entire week of lodgings, and you were just going to abandon them?" she said in disbelief.

"I have a home in London and two country estates I'm currently 'abandoning', if that's how you intend to interpret things," he replied. "Of those, the least of my allegiance is to Marrywell."

"But..." Inspiration struck. "Didn't you say you plan to marry me off posthaste? And yet, you do *not* plan to ferry me about London? In that case, wouldn't it be more expeditious to remain here, at a week-long matchmaking festival, in which unmarried gentlemen from all corners of England have come to find a bride?"

She knew her logic was unassailable. The horror on his handsome face indicated *he* knew it, as well.

"I don't intend to gad about with you anywhere. London or Marrywell or otherwise," he said coldly.

"I'll attend the events on my own," she suggested.

"A young lady of good breeding would never dream of attending a social event without a proper chaperone."

"I think we've established that the only one of those words that describes me is 'young', and even that's only true for three more weeks. I've no idea how to be a lady, and doubt my breeding comes close to meeting your exacting standards."

"All the more reason you shan't show your face anywhere without a chaperone."

"I'll ask Aunt Stapleton to chaperone."

"You will not. She's old and tired and already stated her desire to return home after the tart-and-pie competition tomorrow morning."

"Then I'll ask..." her words faded.

He sighed. "You don't know anyone else."

"John Coachman?" she said hopefully.

"Good God." The earl recoiled. "You really *can't* be left to make decisions on your own. Very well. We'll stay until the tart-and-pie competition."

Matilda clapped her hands. "Thank you!"

"I'm not doing it for you," he muttered. "I'm doing

it for me. Find a husband fast, or I'll betroth you to whomever wins the tart-and-pie competition."

She patted his arm. "We'll have a splendid time. You'll see."

He gingerly plucked her hand from his arm and dropped it back in her lap. "Rule number one: never touch me."

"But I touched you when we were behind the—"

"Temporary insanity," he interrupted firmly. "I've since recovered."

"No touching means no kisses?"

"You're catching on. No kissing me or any man, unless the banns have been read or you're married to him. Understood?"

"Understood," she parroted blandly. After all, one could *understand* a rule without having the least intention of following it.

Her guardian might think that finding a mate for Matilda was his new mission, but she had a new project of her own: the Earl of Gilbourne.

She would coax a smile to his lips if it was the last thing she did.

He might think himself incapable of loosening his rigid mores, but he'd done so once, behind the ferns with her. Which meant he was capable of loosening up again. She would simply have to keep poking until she pushed him right over the edge.

"I mean it, Miss Dodd," he said warily. "Do not embarrass me. Behave as if you were a lady of high station tomorrow, or you will find yourself back in this carriage if I have to bind your hands and feet and toss you over my shoulder like a trussed pig. Understood?"

"Understood," she assured him. She would behave... exactly how she pleased.

"Rule number two," he continued. "All my rules

are law. If I tell you to do something, you do it. If I tell you not to do something, you do not do it. You shall not question my judgment, my motivation, or my aims. You obey. Understood, Miss Dodd?"

"Understood," she said again.

How long would it take him to realize *understood* was not the same as *Yes, my lord and master, your every wish is my command and great honor*? Could it really be that, as a peer of the realm, everyone he came in contact with obeyed his whims regardless of circumstance, personal preference, or basic humanity?

If so, then bully for them, but Matilda did not intend to allow anything or anyone to hold her back. Not an interminable list of rules, whether the Earl of Gilbourne's or those of Polite Society. And definitely not the repressive walls erected by her new guardian.

To begin with, they were going to be *friends*.

"You needn't call me Miss Dodd," she informed him in her friendliest, gentlest, most earnest tones. "I am Matilda."

"You are Miss Dodd," he snapped.

"And you?" she continued breezily, as if he hadn't spoken. "What do I call you?"

"You may say, 'my lord'."

She clasped her hands to her chest and grinned at him beneath fluttering lashes. "You're saying… you're mine?"

He grimaced as if in pain. "Or *Gilbourne*. You may call me Gilbourne."

"May I call you Gil?"

His eyes flashed. "No."

"Gilly?" she tried again.

"*No.*"

"Titus?"

He glared at her.

"Should've been 'tight arse'," she murmured. "More apt."

"Miss Dodd," he said icily. "Please understand that I have agreed to provide nothing more than the bare minimum. I shall give you food and shelter and keep you alive until you turn twenty-one or attract a suitor, whichever comes first."

"And after that?"

A muscle twitched at his temple. "After that, we never see each other again. Or even cross each other's minds."

"Understood," she said sweetly.

It was the Earl of Gilbourne who didn't yet understand. Once Matilda came into her inheritance, she would no longer need him.

But he was going to wish he still had *her*.

CHAPTER 6

When the coach-and-four rolled to a stop in front of Marrywell's storied Blushing Maid Inn, Matilda gathered up her reticule stuffed with diced, candied peels. She'd been popping them into her mouth one by one, trying to put all her focus on their singular texture and flavor, to distract herself from the scowling, hulking, abominably attractive earl at her side.

When he handed her out of the carriage, her fingers nearly melted into his palm. The brief contact was over in the blink of an eye. He clearly had not exaggerated his disinclination for physical contact with her, which only made the brief touch of his gloved hand against hers seem all the more potent and heady.

Lord Gilbourne tipped his chin toward a second large black carriage drawing to a halt right behind the earl's elegant coach-and-four. "Your trunk has arrived. I'll have it and your lady's maid brought to your room."

Matilda blinked. "My trunk and my what?"

The driver opened the door, and a robust red-haired girl a few years younger than Matilda bounded out of the carriage. She glanced at the busy street in obvious confusion. Her eyes widened when she caught sight of Matilda and Lord Gilbourne.

"That's Buttons," said the earl. "Your lady's maid."

Matilda gave her a cautious smile and a little wave of her hand.

Buttons bounded over like a bunny rabbit. "My goodness, your hair! I do love a challenge. Please say I can braid it tonight! I have the perfect tincture to give you the most cunning curls in the morning."

"Er," said Matilda. "I suppose that's fine."

Buttons squealed in delight and bounced on her heels.

Matilda sent a startled glance over her shoulder at the earl.

He shrugged. "I hired her a fortnight ago when my godmother cooked up this codswallop. Buttons might have been bored whilst she awaited your arrival."

An impeccably dressed older gentleman approached behind Buttons. He tilted his head toward Matilda and whispered, "I should react in much the same manner if his lordship would allow me to perform my full duties as well."

"Augustin, my valet," the duke said coldly. "Who is not to speak to Miss Dodd without express leave to do so."

"You have my permission to speak to me any time you please," Matilda said without hesitation. "All of you do. I'm not one to stand on ceremony, and I'm sure I'm no better than any of you."

"Oh my," said Buttons, darting an alarmed glance toward Lord Gilbourne.

"Oh my is right," said Augustin, his eyes twinkling with mischief. "This *is* going to get interesting."

"Have the footmen take the trunks upstairs," the

earl commanded. "I'll use the same room as before. We shall install Miss Dodd in the bedchamber farthest from mine."

"How many bedchambers are *in* your suite?" Matilda asked in wonder.

"Milord has rented half of the first floor," Augustin answered.

"Even ill-mannered servants need a place to sleep," Lord Gilbourne said curtly.

Augustin cupped a hand over his mouth to whisper to Matilda, "And our prickly employer would never send us up to the attic with everyone else's servants."

"Because an earl's servants rank higher?" Matilda whispered back.

The valet shook his head. "Because attics are cramped and hot and unbearable. Milord may try to deny his compassionate nature, but if one pays close enough attention—"

"Enough whispering," the earl snapped. "Have you no job to do?"

Augustin gave Matilda a wink, then hurried to help the footmen into the hotel and up the stairs with the traveling trunks.

Matilda followed behind, with the earl at her side and Buttons at her heels.

As soon as the door to the earl's suite was secured behind them, Lord Gilbourne turned to Matilda. "Buttons is to accompany you at all times. It is her chaperonage, along with our impersonal guardian-and-ward relationship that makes it acceptable for us to sleep under the same roof."

"Is there such a thing as an impersonal relationship?" she asked, remembering their kiss. "And even if so, are you certain we're in one?"

"All of my dealings with others are impersonal.

Do not fool yourself into believing otherwise. The moment you reach your majority, I shall wash my hands of you."

Rude.

"Don't you worry," she shot back. "There's no manner in which I'd rather spend my birthday than giving myself the present of leaving *you*."

Gilbourne's jaw tightened. "Good. Then our wishes align."

She crossed her arms and lifted her chin. "Good."

The earl stalked off without another word.

Matilda wished she could call him back. Her words had been spoken in hurt and anger and embarrassment. His sharp dismissal of her in front of the servants had felt unnecessary and cruel.

Perhaps Augustin was wrong, and the earl was the sort of lord who considered servants no more human than candlesticks, if he thought of them at all.

Or maybe he thought *Matilda* had no more feelings than a piece of pewter.

She was certainly starting to suspect it was true of him.

Matilda turned to her new lady's maid. "What have you been doing whilst you awaited my arrival?"

"Reading books from the earl's private collection," Buttons answered. "It's mostly been a paid holiday."

Oh.

"An absolute tyrant," Matilda murmured. "I suppose I can see Augustin's point."

The earl had a heart after all. Unfortunately, if Lord Gilbourne wasn't a monster... it meant he simply didn't like Matilda.

"Come with me," said Buttons. "Allow me to help ready you for bed."

Matilda followed obediently. She still wasn't used to being helped with anything. When her parents had been alive, they'd all contributed their part. Father, with the maintenance of their cottage and its humble grounds, Matilda and her mother with the cooking and cleaning.

After their deaths, when she'd gone to live with Aunt Stapleton, Matilda's new guest chamber was far finer than anything she'd experienced before. Nonetheless, she spent her year of mourning in such deep grief that she barely registered her surroundings. There had been no need for a lady's maid. Matilda rarely left her bed. When she took meals at all, she did so alone in her room, and never once ventured outside her great-aunt's Shropshire home.

When the year of mourning was through, Aunt Stapleton insisted Matilda return to a world of color and activity.

And now here she was, soaking in a perfumed bath whilst a servant washed her hair. It was absolutely decadent.

Matilda could scarcely believe that Gilbourne had gone so far as to hire a personal lady's maid for the brief period whilst his unwanted ward awaited her twenty-first birthday.

His idea of providing the bare minimum was clearly wildly different from hers. She made a mental note to thank him for his thoughtfulness. And to tell him, effusively, just how sweet and kindhearted she found his actions.

He was certain to hate every word.

CHAPTER 7

*T*he next morning was no less luxurious an experience. Rather than shimmy into an old walking dress on her own, Matilda stood in place like a living doll as Buttons happily dressed her in... well, one of Matilda's old gowns. Humble attire had never bothered Matilda before, because she'd never had any occasion to dress any finer.

Now that she was in the middle of Marrywell in the height of a matchmaking festival, she wished she at least had a new ribbon for her hair. Not all the merrymakers were wealthy lords and ladies, but even the farmers' daughters presented themselves in their best light.

Buttons read her mind.

"You sit here on this stool," her new lady's maid commanded, "and allow me the honor of properly arranging your hair. Here's a looking glass, so that you can watch the transformation."

Matilda sat, and accepted the handheld round mirror.

It wasn't cold enough to require a roaring fire, but Buttons stoked a few low flames in the grate. She dangled a pair of curling tongs just out of reach until the metal heated, then set to work turning Matilda's mass of thick, dense hair into sleek, symmetrical ringlets.

It was enthralling and deeply exciting. It also took *forever*.

"I presume such attentions are only for special occasions?" she asked.

"Every time a lady exits her chambers is a special occasion," Buttons replied.

"I'm not a lady," Matilda reminded her.

"Madam, you're the ward of a wealthy earl who has rented one of the finest suites and hired an experienced lady's maid away from her prior post in order to ensure you present yourself as befitting your position. It certainly sounds like you're a privileged young lady to me."

It sounded that way to Matilda, as well. The thought was dizzying. "Wait. Lord Gilbourne stole you away from some other employer?"

"Do you think a man like your earl would entrust his ward's public appearance to an unemployed lay-about with second-rate skills?"

"No," Matilda admitted. "I imagine Lord Gilbourne is used to the very best, and having every wish granted. Speaking of which, he said he would see me in the morning. Won't he be wondering what's taking me so long?"

"Ton gentlemen know exactly what's taking so long," Buttons informed her. "Many of their valets require more time than lady's maids do. Beau Brummell's morning toilette drags on for hours. I am renowned for my expediency."

Good Lord, this was *quick*? "You mean I'll be ready before Lord Gilbourne is?"

"Oh, he's been ready since dawn," Buttons said breezily. "Rumor has it, he doesn't even allow his

valet to shave his whiskers, preferring to do everything himself."

"But if he's been up for hours... are we keeping
him from going down to breakfast? Or has he already
done so, and I'm to dine on my own?"

"Neither. Milord does not permit himself a single
morsel of food until he has responded to all of his
correspondence and completed any outstanding
tasks related to his committees in the House of
Lords. I shouldn't be surprised if you find yourself
the one waiting on *him*."

But when Matilda emerged from her bedchamber, the earl was indeed standing alone and ready in
the small parlor where she had last seen him. His jaw
was freshly shaven, and his hands clasped behind his
back. Unlike the previous night, Lord Gilbourne was
not in evening wear, but the lack did nothing to hide
his handsomeness or diminish his larger-than-life
presence.

His boots were spotless, the shiny black leather
rising almost to his knees. His powerful thighs were
encased in skintight buckskins. His wide shoulders
and thick arms, tailored to perfection in a well-cut
coat of olive green. A sliver of emerald waistcoat was
visible beneath the sharp white folds of his cravat,
above which...

Well, above which, scowled the earl.

His face was just as arresting as it had been the
night before. Now that broad daylight replaced the
flickering candles and evening shadows of the
crowded ballroom, Matilda could see every detail all
the more clearly. A strong jaw and stubborn chin.
Cheekbones to die for. Dark brows slashing beneath
a wide forehead. A web of raised scars stretching
across half of his face. Firm lips, unsmiling... But, as

she knew from personal experience, that cynical mouth was eminently kissable.

He gazed at her impassively, his eyes not dipping once to review her shabby-genteel attire, nor raising up toward the towering cornucopia of ringlets befitting a royal princess. His gaze did stray to her lips, ever so briefly, as if he too recalled in perfect detail the stolen minutes in which their mouths had been locked together.

"Come," he commanded. "We shall take breakfast in the dining room."

"Thank you," she blurted out. "I know you didn't ask for a ward, but you've already provided more than I ever expected. My room is lovely, as is Buttons. She's my first full-time lady's maid, dedicated just to me, and the sensation is rather—"

His jaw flexed. "Are you always this loquacious?"

Her teeth clicked together in shock. She'd anticipated his discomfort with her thanks, but to not even offer a polite *It was my pleasure…* Very well, she must simply be conversationalist enough for both of them.

Loquacious? He had no idea what she was capable of.

"What a beautiful day," she chirped, despite the rain coming down in torrents and the wind rattling the panes of glass in their whitewashed wooden frames. "I adore spring above all seasons, not just because of all the flowers that blossom and bloom, but also because it feels like the world itself begins anew. We get to watch it grow and thrive."

He stalked toward the stairs. "It's a miserable day."

She hurried to keep up. "It reminds me of you."

At this, he did send her a sharp look over his shoulder. "Are you calling me miserable?"

"You're the one who said today was miserable," she replied blithely. "*I* said it was beautiful. The skies may be gray now, but they won't be for long. There's already open pockets between the clouds where the sun is starting to poke through. I'd wager we won't even need an umbrella by the time we're through with breakfast."

"Proper young ladies don't wager," he said tersely.

"I've always yearned to be wildly improper," she said dreamily. "This might be my best chance. Before, I rarely had occasion to leave our small farm. Aunt Stapleton resides in a much larger house in a much larger town, but as I was in mourning, I never left my bedchamber. This is the first opportunity I've ever had in my entire life to—"

At the bottom of the stairs, a Blushing Maid Inn footman stood at the open doorway to the busy public dining area, hovering at the ready to show guests to their seats.

Matilda curled her fingers around Lord Gilbourne's elbow.

He jerked out of her grasp as if she'd doused him with acid.

"Rule one," he said coldly. "No touching. Rule two: You do as I say, not as you please. Need I repeat the rules again, or has your provincial brain understood this time?"

Matilda's throat tightened as she dropped her hands back to her sides. "I understand."

"Good." He turned to the inn's footman. "Two, please."

"There was no need to come down to make the request," stammered the footman. "It is no problem at all to send up an extra meal."

"That is kind of you," the earl replied, as if he were currently being filleted at knifepoint. "However, we shall break our fast in the dining room this morning, if you don't mind."

"Oh. *Oh.* Of course." The footman's eyes widened as though having difficulty parsing the earl's words, but he quickly collected himself. "If you'll come with me, milord."

"They weren't expecting us?" Matilda whispered.

"No. Upon my arrival, I gave explicit instruction that all meals were to be sent up to the suite at precise hours, and that I otherwise was not to be interrupted."

"Dining with others is an interruption?"

"Everything that takes me away from my desk is an interruption."

"Then why accompany me downstairs at all?"

"I am still asking myself that question." The earl waited as the footman helped Matilda into a wooden chair before taking his own seat.

"Coffee or tea?" asked the footman.

"Tea, please," Matilda answered.

The earl inclined his head. "Two."

The footman bowed. "Straight away. Your breakfasts shall arrive shortly."

"Thank you." The earl did not look thankful. He crossed his arms over his wide chest and glared at the bustling dining room as though willing it to burst into flames.

"Do you hate all public places or just all hungry diners?" Matilda enquired.

"All public places," he answered flatly. "And all unnecessary conversations."

"Why not order me to take my meals in my room, as you do?"

He glowered at her rather than respond.

"Because you're kindhearted and considerate by nature," she answered for both of them. "How sweet."

He looked horrified.

"How temporary," he corrected her. "We depart as

soon as the competition ends. When we reach London, my usual habits will resume. And as soon as you reach your majority or land a suitor, whichever comes first, I shall have one fewer annoyance to worry about."

She beamed at him. "You worry about me? You really are the sweetest man. In fact, you've helped me to see that if I ever do choose a suitor, I shall not accept less of a true gentleman than you yourself."

"*When* you take a suitor," he said repressively, "it will likely be the one and only sad fool desperate enough to—"

"Two hot breakfasts." A serving maid with a heavy tray began to set a series of small plates on the table. "Eggs, kippers, toast, marmalade, fresh fruit—oh, and here comes your tea. Thank you, Hilda. There you are, then. Enjoy your meal."

Matilda expected Gilbourne to shovel as much food into his mouth as possible, so as to avoid any further conversation with her.

Instead, he simply lowered his baleful glare from her face to the hot dishes on the table, as though they'd been placed there with no other aim but to vex him with their very existence.

She helped herself to a healthy portion of everything, keeping up a constant patter about the smell of fresh bread, the joy of orange marmalade, and the satisfying saltiness of a nice hot kipper.

The earl looked as though he'd rather bury himself alive than suffer through an additional moment in this dining room. He consumed a single piece of dry toast.

As soon as Matilda put down her fork, he shot out of his chair. "That's over, then."

She folded her napkin before she rose. "Off to the festivities, are we? How delightful."

"I intend to return to the peace and quiet of my private chambers until the hour for the ridiculous tart-and-pie competition arrives. You shall wait in your own chambers, silently, until I summon you." He stalked from the dining room toward the stairs.

"But I thought you *wanted* to marry me off."

He paused before taking the first step up. "Your point?"

"My point is that there are significantly fewer eligible suitors inside my empty guest chamber than there are roaming the grounds of the annual Marry-well matchmaking festival."

He ground his teeth, then glanced over her shoulder. "Stay close behind, Buttons."

Matilda spun about in surprise. "Buttons! When did you sneak downstairs?"

"I've been behind you this whole time," her lady's maid replied. "I'm to keep you in my sights and to stay out of yours as much as possible."

"You're doing an excellent job," Matilda marveled. "Did you at least get breakfast?"

"She ate with the servants," Gilbourne interrupted, striding toward the exit. "If we're to attend these infernal festivities, let us not put off the inevitable."

"You're referring to merrymaking?" Matilda asked as she skipped up to his side, careful not to touch him.

"I'm referring to you. Ideally betrothed and off my hands." He paused to turn and address the innkeeper behind the counter. "Where is the highest concentration of eligible bachelors at this hour?"

"At this hour?" the innkeeper repeated with a smile. "Most likely at the follies in the center of the labyrinth. Always a crush by the pond at any time of the day."

"Marvelous," the earl muttered.

A footman rushed to open the door for them. Outside, the driver of a carriage parked in front of the hotel shook the last of the rain from his top hat.

Matilda was right—the sun *had* come out! She grinned up at Lord Gilbourne in triumph.

He was not attending to her. The sight of the horse and carriage—and all of the other horses and carriages clogging the road—appeared to have put him on edge. As he forced himself to meld with the crowd of early morning merrymakers wending their way toward the pleasure gardens, his posture was stiff, his gait wooden, and his expression resolute.

"This will be fun," she assured him.

He grimaced. "I'm afraid of that."

CHAPTER 8

*T*he moment Matilda and Lord Gilbourne stepped away from the street and into the shady green silence of the towering hedgerow labyrinth, the earl seemed to become an entirely different person, right before her eyes.

Everything about him relaxed. His muscles, his posture, his tight jaw and clenched teeth. All of that vanished, leaving behind a dapper man who looked as though he hadn't a care in the world. Instead of hulking at her side, all thick arms and legs and angry scowls, his arms swung loose and his legs ambled without hurry. He wasn't *smiling*—the earl never smiled—but even the scarred half of his face looked peaceful and... friendly?

Matilda gazed at the transformation in awe. "Are the botanical gardens your favorite part of Marrywell?"

"I wouldn't know. I've never been to Marrywell before." This was said with equanimity, rather than irritation.

"Then... You don't know how to navigate the maze to arrive at the follies?"

"I haven't the slightest notion," he confirmed with something astoundingly close to good cheer.

"Are you simply an aficionado of nature?" she insisted, cognizant that her impertinence could flare his temper at any moment.

"I wouldn't know that, either," he replied without a frown. "I never leave my study, if I can help it."

She stared at him in wonder. He was in a town he did not know, bumbling through a complex maze whose solution eluded them... and he was as relaxed as a kitten napping beneath the morning sun?

What the devil had got into him?

Or—a sudden thought occurred to her—was *this* his natural state, and the usual biting misanthropy a secondary effect of external stressors?

Five minutes ago, she would have counted herself as one of those stressors, but at the moment, he didn't seem bothered at all to be strolling down shady hedgerow paths at her side, shrugging and turning around gamely whenever they came face-first with a dead end.

Fascinating. She remembered how tense he had become when they'd stepped outside the hotel. The snarl of horse and carriage traffic amid the hordes of pedestrians was overwhelming, particularly to a girl who had been raised in a hamlet the size of a pea, but the earl's reaction had been even more severe.

He refused to leave the peace and quiet of his study.

He preferred to take all meals alone in his chamber.

The noise and the congestion did not simply annoy him. He must *hate* it. Viscerally. The same way she could not stand the sight or even the mention of spiders. The violent panics her phobia caused were beyond her control. And it wasn't a frivolous overreaction—her body's reactions to bites were far worse than the average person's. If Gilbourne reacted to fashionable crushes as she reacted to a spiderweb, then the man deserved sainthood for coming to collect her at the height of one of the biggest fairs in England.

She was dying to ask further questions to prove or disprove her theory. But she despised *talking* about spiders almost as much as spiders themselves. Nor did she wish to risk spoiling the cease-fire by bringing up the very topic he most wished to forget.

"These are my first botanical gardens, as well," she offered, then glanced up at Lord Gilbourne cautiously.

Normally, such a comment would be met with a frosty glare, and perhaps a snide comment about loquaciousness or unnecessary babble.

Instead of any of that, he replied, "Oh, it's not my first garden. My family and I spent many afternoons in Hyde Park and Vauxhall when I was small."

He could have knocked Matilda over with a feather.

Two pleasant sentences in a row! Offering unsolicited personal details about himself and his past! Without a single glare!

The Earl of Gilbourne was not nearly as dreadful a beast as everyone seemed to think. They simply came in contact with him in the precise circumstances guaranteed to put him at odds with the world: crowded streets, crowded ballrooms, possibly even the crowded House of Lords. If she was right, then fulfilling his comital duties to Parliament was nothing short of daily torture during the long eight months of the legislative season.

In fact, Parliament was still in session. By being

here instead of there, Matilda was taking the earl away from important responsibilities.

Yet he looked content to stroll through the cool, shady hedgerows for hours if need be.

"I'd like to be friends," she blurted out.

He sent her a look. Not a cruel look. A confused look. "I don't have friends."

"That's where you're wrong. It's already done. We're friends now. No sense fighting facts. There's nothing you can do to stop it."

He looked amused, rather than annoyed, at this. "The other party need not accept the offer?"

"Usually there is no formal offer," she explained. "Friendships happen by themselves, oftentimes wholly by accident. It would be highly unusual to draw up some sort of official contract outlining specific rules of engagement."

"And yet there must be rules," he said. "Everything has rules."

"You could first-name me," she offered. "Friends often do that. I'm Matilda. Try it."

"I shall refrain, Miss Dodd."

"If 'Matilda' is too long, you can call me 'Tilda.'"

He shook his head. "No."

"Just 'Da,'" she suggested.

"No."

"Or 'Till,'" she offered.

"*No.* Nor will I call you 'Ma', Miss Dodd."

Three *no*es in a row, yet he still wasn't scowling.

Matilda was positively giddy. If this kept up—

They turned another corner and the magic spell evaporated like a burst bubble. Noise and sunlight spilt through a wide gap in the hedgerows. They'd reached the center of the labyrinth.

Huzzah.

The change in Lord Gilbourne was instantaneous.

ERICA RIDLEY

The lines in his forehead were back, the clench of his jaw, the tic in his scarred temple. His posture was tense, wary, and dangerous. A surly bear minding its own business who would not hesitate to lash out at the slightest provocation.

"It seems we found the way out," Matilda said, just to fill the silence.

The earl was clearly back to not speaking again. No doubt too busy grinding his teeth into dust to bother with unnecessary small talk.

His guard was up—and so was hers, if for a different reason.

She was not used to rubbing shoulders with the beau monde. Yes, yes, the Earl of Gilbourne was by definition a lord, but he was also her guardian, and legally saddled with her, like it or not. He could not reject her.

All these other people... Matilda couldn't even tell which ones *were* haut ton, and which ones were simply wealthy enough to dress the part. She wasn't the only country-bred miss present, but all the others seemed to have arrived at the follies in big families or large groups of friends.

Picnic blankets encircled the large pond in the center, the blankets themselves barely visible beneath all the colorful skirts of fine gowns and the chattering, smiling faces of so many people.

Matilda wanted to be one of them so badly, she could taste it. She longed for a big family. Make that *any* family. She missed her parents so much, her insides were hollow with the loss. She had never gone a single day without their love and conversation and good-night kisses on her forehead. Not until the fever came and turned her country paradise into hell.

She wished she had a huge group of friends. The sort who would spy her standing awkwardly at the exit of the labyrinth and yell out, "Matilda's here!" in undisguised delight. The sort of friends that would scramble up from their blankets and run to her in their eagerness, arms spread wide for a hug.

She wanted to be seen. To be wanted. To be accepted. To be enough.

But no one even looked in her direction.

CHAPTER 9

"*R*eady to go back to the hotel?" Lord Gilbourne asked.

"No." Matilda rolled back her shoulders. "I'm about to make friends."

He stepped away from the mouth of the labyrinth. "I doubt it's as simple as you think."

Matilda didn't think it was simple at all. She'd implied so to him earlier because *she* was easy to be friends with. Just say *good morning* or *how do you do* and Matilda would happily return the favor. She'd grown up in the sort of house where the postman or the milkmaid might stay for a biscuit or a cup of tea before continuing on their way. Matilda could make friends with a bumblebee.

And could she make friends here in Marrywell, too.

"Stay here and scowl at everyone if you like," she told the earl. "I'll show you how it's done."

He crossed his arms, leaned against a tree, and closed his eyes as if taking a nap. "I'm enthralled."

Matilda glanced over her shoulder.

Buttons was still hanging back in the shadows of the labyrinth, careful not to intrude. Blast.

Matilda was not above begging for intrusion. She made large *please-come-here* gestures until Buttons stepped close enough for Matilda to flash out her arm and link elbows, as if they were bosom friends out for a morning promenade.

"Stop it, miss," Buttons hissed, appalled. "It isn't seemly."

Matilda hesitated. She was holding onto Buttons for dear life, but she was also on a mission to make friends with everyone else in the gardens. A task that apparently could not be accomplished unless one was *seemly*, whatever that meant.

"His lordship will give me the sack if my actions cause gossip," Buttons added. "We're not to embarrass him."

Matilda gritted her teeth and dropped her lady's maid's arm. She didn't want to be the subject of ridicule *or* the cause of Buttons losing her post. She must do this alone.

"Stay close," she whispered, and inched forward into the crowd of people.

So many people. Hundreds of them. Milling about the pond, picnicking around the border, crossing the bridge, climbing the follies, smelling the flowers.

None of them gave Matilda a second glance.

She beamed at them all anyway. Said "Good day!" and "How do you do!" so brightly and so often that her throat grew hoarse and her cheeks ached from smiling so hard.

No one said anything in reply.

Matilda overheard snippets from dozens of conversations. Horse races, a brewer's field, pudding flavors, seven maidens fair.

She edged closer to a group of young women about her own age, in hopes of blending in and being welcomed.

"But *Oldfield*, Bernice?" asked a red-haired girl with a shudder.

"He's old, all right," said another girl in a big yellow bonnet.

"And he's a viscount," said Bernice, the finest dressed of them all. "His title is all that matters."

"He's spoken for," said the red-haired girl. "I would've married his heir."

"Medford already married someone else," said Yellow Bonnet.

"I shall birth *new* heirs, you featherbrains," said Bernice. "Heirs presumptive can be displaced. Think bigger. My son will inherit the title."

Ugh. "Is there no unmarried lord not old enough to be our father?" asked the red-headed girl.

"Well..." her friend said slowly. "There's the Marquess of Creslow, isn't there? And the Earl of Gilbourne."

"Gilbourne!" Bernice scoffed. "He never attends social events."

"He's attending this social event at this very moment," said the red-haired girl.

"Turn around and see," said Yellow Bonnet. "He's sleeping against a tree trunk next to the labyrinth."

Bernice whipped about—and came face-to-face with Matilda.

"You're in my way," she snapped. "*Move.*"

Matilda stepped aside reflexively, although she was not eager to share her guardian with this young lady.

"He *is* here," Bernice breathed. "And an *earl*."

"And a monster," said yellow bonnet with a shiver. "Just the thought of that face anywhere near mine..."

"He's rude and cruel and coldhearted," agreed the red-haired girl. "I couldn't bear a minuet with him, much less a marriage."

"I could for the title of countess," said Bernice. "He'll do."

Matilda couldn't believe what she was hearing. That was it? End of necessary qualifications? Gilbourne won battles before they began, simply because he'd been born a lord. This woman wanted to marry him based on literally nothing else. She didn't even *like* him. His title was all it took.

"But... Gilbourne?" yellow bonnet said dubiously. "He frightens everyone who steps into his path."

"Rich as Croesus, but doesn't spend a shilling," added the red-haired girl. "Think of your pin money. Or lack thereof."

"And he's the terror of the House of Lords," added yellow bonnet.

Bernice frowned. "Is he speaker of the house?"

"No," yellow bonnet answered. "Gilbourne has no need for elected titles in order to have the last word. His arguments are unbeatable. All the other lords want him on their committees because whoever's side he opposes always loses."

"You are *such* a bluestocking," the red-haired girl muttered. "Who cares about Parliament? The main point is that Gilbourne is a boring curmudgeon. He won't take tea with others, much less attend a ball or a party."

"I don't care that he's an ugly, off-putting beast," said Bernice. "I'll marry him and rule the female half of London."

"You're the one who's off-putting," Matilda burst out. "It's your manners that are ugly. He's a perfectly lovely man—"

"*Gilbourne?*" sputtered yellow bonnet in disbelief.

"—who does not deserve being gossiped about and denigrated in such a presumptuous manner. You don't know the first thing about him—"

63

"I know I'm going to marry him," Bernice said as if bored.

"—because *if you did*," Matilda finished, "you'd know he's too discerning to waste his lordly breath on the likes of you!"

Red-hair and yellow bonnet gasped in shock.

"Who do you think you are?" Bernice snarled.

"Miss Matilda Dodd," she answered.

Bernice's smile was terrifying. "I suppose you think *you're* woman enough for the Earl of Gilbourne, little orphan?"

"I..." The fire dissolved from Matilda. This lady knew who she was?

"You're a poor relation to him, and a poor choice in bride for any man here," Bernice continued blandly.

"If you didn't know he was here, how do you know I'm his ward?" Matilda stammered.

"Because I know everything about everyone," Bernice replied, leaning so close that Matilda was forced to take a step back. "My mother plays whist with your godmother. I didn't know who you were when you first came creeping up—everyone tries to be part of my circle—but once you defended your guardian so pitiably, I suspected." She cast her gaze up and down Matilda's clothing. "Not that those pathetic rags leave any doubt as to the quality of your up-bringing."

Matilda's mouth fell open and her fists balled. "Don't you dare... M-my parents..."

"Are dead, yes I know. Boo hoo. Run along then, and cry over their gravestones. This is a match-making festival. You're ruining the atmosphere for those of us capable of making matches."

Red-hair and yellow bonnet didn't hide their giggles.

Matilda's temper flared, but she took a deep breath. "I didn't come here to pick a fight. I came here to make friends—"

"Make them with slugs your own status," snapped Bernice. "The rest of us are busy, from now until infinity. Now get out of my face before I scream, and bring your strapping guardian running to my rescue."

Throat tight, Matilda walked stiffly back to the tree near the mouth of the labyrinth with her pride hurt and her spirits crushed.

"Make friends with everyone already?" the earl asked without opening his eyes.

She opened her mouth. Not to answer, but to shovel diced bits of lemon and orange peels. She tried her hardest to derive composure from each cherished burst of flavor.

The earl opened his eyes. "Good God, I can smell that from here. Are you eating an entire orchard?"

"Candied peels." Her voice shook. "Do you want one?"

"It looks like they're all already in your mouth."

"I eat one whenever I'm nervous or need a lift in spirits," she said defensively.

"One fistful?" he said dryly, then pushed away from the tree trunk. "*Now* can we return to the hotel?"

"Yes." Matilda's shoulders sagged with defeat. "Please."

CHAPTER 10

*T*itus finally took an easy breath when he and Miss Dodd stepped back into the private serenity of the labyrinth.

He had done his duty as a guardian by accompanying her to the center as she'd wished, and now he could not be more eager to leave the chaos behind and return to the relative safety of his hotel suite.

It wasn't that he'd expected any particular calamity to strike. It was that one never knew. Accidents were unpredictable by definition. They could strike at any time. There was no foolproof method to avoid disaster, but one could lower the likelihood significantly by avoiding dangerous activities and large crowds. And why not be careful? Avoiding was the easiest thing in the world.

Or at least, it had been. Until a surprise ward had dropped in his lap. Er, not his lap. Beside him. He *wanted* her in his lap. And on her back, and in his bed. Which was all the more reason to keep her at arm's length. The only thing more dangerous than crowds was *caring* about a specific person therein. Much safer to keep one's heart ice cold and locked away in a secure vault.

"Do you remember the way out?" she asked.

"No."

He hadn't tried to memorize the route. If anything, he'd done his best not to apply logic and spatial cues to the maze. On the way in, expediency would have meant joining the throngs of merrymakers all the sooner. And on the way out, to exit the labyrinth meant spilling back into the busy street with all its carts and carriages and horses and pedestrians.

Of course, *not* memorizing the route meant he must now spend more time with Miss Dodd. Whom he was definitely keeping at arm's length. Or at least elbow length. For his own sake, as much as for hers.

"How was your nap?" she enquired.

"I didn't have one."

She slid a glance at him. "Were you watching me?"

"No."

That was the real reason he'd kept his eyes closed. When they were open and Miss Dodd was in view, Titus could not force his gaze anywhere else. She was like a bright summer day in human form, projecting rainbows and sunshine wherever she went.

Except she was looking a bit more like a spring squall at the moment. A gust of wind, a dash of rain. Her usually smiling face was pensive, and her hand kept tracking back and forth between her reticule and her mouth, as tiny candied orange peel square after tiny candied lemon peel square disappeared from view.

"Did… your time at the follies not go according to plan?"

"No," she said softly. "Things did not go to plan."

Titus was sorry he asked, because now that he knew, he felt bad about leaving her to navigate the crowd on her own. And he was angry that he felt bad. He had neither asked nor wished to be in such a position. Having an unplanned dependent was disruption enough. The last thing he needed was to care about *her* feelings and hopes.

The only solution was to marry her off without delay. Rid himself of temptation.

Of course, he was currently in the act of leading her away from the predetermined location where large quantities of bride-seeking gentlemen had come to congregate. Talk about one's desires not going to plan.

"Everyone seems to know who you are," she said.

He was not surprised. "Most have had Debrett's Peerage drilled into them since birth. And my face *is* difficult to forget."

"Why should anyone want to?"

He stared at her sharply. Ever since the accident, no one but his godmother could meet his eye for long. Passers-by blanched and scurried away upon catching sight of him. Even in the House of Lords, his fellow peers kept their focus somewhere above his top hat or over his shoulder rather than on the raised white scars puckering half of Titus's face.

But Miss Dodd's warm brown gaze never strayed from meeting his eyes with earnest confusion, as if his countenance was no more remarkable than anyone else's, and possibly even... tolerable.

"You must be jesting," he said flatly.

"Oh, your scars?" she said, as if his disfigurement was no more noteworthy than a stray freckle or a charming dimple. "Of course I can see them. But who hasn't been wounded, visibly or otherwise?"

He glared at her in consternation. Not only was she the first non-medical person to openly acknowledge the damage wrought to his face, she dismissed it as though it meant nothing.

They meant everything.

The scars she could see were only the beginning. His careful layers of well-tailored clothing hid much more. And every line, every welt, every still-tender ache reminded him sharply of all he had lost.

"My disfigurement," he bit out, "is significantly more real than whatever invisible wounds you imagine that *you* possess."

"Is it?" she said softly, then blinked and glanced away.

There. He'd got what he wanted. She was no longer looking at him. His jaw clenched. That *was* what he wanted. Wasn't it?

They walked along in uncomfortable silence.

"The flowers were nice," she offered presently. "Didn't you think?"

Titus had never been more grateful for inane small talk. Of course the flowers were nice. These were the largest botanical gardens in England. Four hundred hectares, nearly as grand as Versailles. No one could find fault with something so beautiful.

He was glad she was talking to him again. And angry he'd noticed or cared that she'd stopped.

"I prefer the indoors to the outdoors," he informed her.

"Is that truly your preference, or merely your custom?"

"Would it be my custom if it wasn't my preference?"

She lifted a shoulder. "Humans do all sorts of things out of habit that are neither their fondest wish nor in their best interest."

"Commoners perhaps," he said, knowing he was coming off as insufferable and priggish, and hopeful his bad behavior would drive the prior wedge back between them. "I, however, am an earl, and need not conform to anyone's wishes but my own."

Her expression was infuriatingly close to a smirk. "Is that why you now find yourself guardian to a ward? My presence in your life was your sole and fervent desire?"

He scowled at her.

She burst out laughing. "Oh, I'm just having a bit of fun with you. It's not every day that a country miss finds herself—*ahhh! Haughhh!*"

Miss Dodd began to thrash about as if an invisible heavy net had been cast down upon her from the heavens. Her anguished cries of undiluted panic were dry and guttural and terrified.

Titus was totally at a loss as to what was happening. "What is it?"

"Get it off! Get it off me! *Get it!*" She spun and flailed, swiping at her face and spitting and crying.

He felt utterly helpless in the face of her distress. "Get... what exactly?"

"The spider! The spider! The—" She began to dry heave, still scrubbing at her face and skin and clothing.

He grabbed her by the shoulders. She fought against his grip like a wild thing. He held her still.

"Let me look at you," he commanded, in the cold, carrying authoritarian voice he used to silence his objectors in Parliament.

She froze, not even breathing, only the glassiness of her panicked eyes betraying the violence with which her heart pumped beneath her bodice.

He inspected her as quickly and as thoroughly as he was able, taking care to turn his face and entire body, not just his eyes, so that she could *see* him physically scanning her for signs of a spider.

"You stepped into a spider web?" he asked, his voice low and calm.

Tears leaked from her eyes and she nodded miserably.

He ran his hands down her shoulders and arms, conspicuously flinging away absolutely nothing. Any dregs of the web that had brushed against her were now long gone. He cupped her cheeks next. They were splotchy and red. Cold and clammy from tears. Titus wanted to kiss each tear away. He ran the pads of his thumbs over the soft skin instead.

"It's gone now," he said quietly. "Do you hear me? There's no spider. It's gone."

She remained solid as a log, then let out a hitching breath, flung her trembling arms tight about his ribs, and sobbed into his cravat.

He let her. And stood there, holding her to him. Patting her back and stroking her hair as if she were a kitten. Or a fragile young woman masquerading as impervious. Perhaps deeply in need of comfort.

At last, she pushed away, wiping her wet cheeks with the back of her hands, her expression abashed. "I'm sorry."

"It was nothing."

"It was mortifying for both of us. And a flagrant violation of rule number one: no touching."

"It's *all right*, Miss Dodd." His fingertips still buzzed from the silkiness of her hair.

She gave him a watery smile. "Surely now, you can first-name me?"

"Miss Dodd—"

"Mattie."

He sighed. "Miss Dodd, really—"

"Mattie the Madwoman."

"No." He smoothed his lapels.

"Mattie the *Mat*woman."

He choked. "Good God, please stop. I'll pay you any sum you ask."

71

She grinned and popped a candied orange peel into her mouth, then held up her significantly depleted reticule. "Pay me in these."

"They'll rot your teeth."

"Have you always been such a spoilsport?" she asked cheekily.

No. "Yes."

"I wonder." She gave him a considering look as she slid another square of diced lemon peel into her mouth.

He could not help but suspect the self-deprecating nicknames were as much a defensive measure as her candied peels. And he wondered if either tactic actually worked.

"Do you… want to talk about it?" he asked.

Her smile fell. "No."

He was so surprised, he nearly tripped over his own feet. The ward who hadn't ceased her endless chatter since the moment she was deposited into his hands did *not* wish to talk about something?

Perhaps there was such a thing as invisible wounds after all.

None of which was his problem, he reminded himself firmly. Miss Dodd would be gone in three weeks. Sooner, if he mustered up a suitor for her. It was best to think of her as a pretty painting on loan from a museum. Beautiful, with a possibly tragic history, and ultimately a possession belonging to someone else. Best kept tucked away in some other room, for safety.

But for now, there was no choice but to finish the maze side-by-side.

CHAPTER 11

"*H*ere." Titus sprinted a few feet ahead of Miss Dodd to scoop up a thin, arm's-length dry branch from the earth. He held it out as if presenting her with a magic sword. "Swing this in front of you as you walk. If there are any other spiderwebs, you'll knock them from the path long before they touch you."

Her face paled further. She did not take the branch. "You think there will be more?"

"No," he said quickly. "That's not what I'm saying. I'm honestly surprised there was one at all, what with the quantity of visitors who tramp through here. Except that we *are* out in the middle of nature, and spiders can weave a web with astonishing speed—"

She swayed. His speech was having the opposite effect than intended.

"There are no more spiders," he told her firmly, imbuing his voice with absolute certainty. "Nonetheless, *I* will carry this branch as though it were a walking stick, swinging it to and fro as we stroll. It's an unnecessary gesture, but cannot hurt. Is that acceptable?"

She nodded gratefully, and fell into step at his side.

Titus could not permit himself to soften toward her. Not now, not ever. He certainly could not allow her to realize the depth of his attraction to her. In part for her beauty, and in part because she was the one person in Christendom not afraid of him.

He wondered if that was because she was orphaned. Perhaps it was difficult to fear a mere human after having faced down death.

Then again, Titus had also been orphaned at a young age, and he feared pretty much everything. Perhaps the most vulnerable aspect of Miss Dodd was not her weakness, but her strength. Keeping the broken pieces together was so much harder than allowing the fractured shards to fall apart.

"When my family caught the fever," she said quietly, "we had no servants. The church delivered meals, but we were too ill to eat, and it was too dangerous for anyone to stay and feed us. Mother and I normally kept the cottage spotless, but with all three members of the household confined to our sickbeds, our pristine home quickly attracted dust and insects."

Titus had never been without servants, and could not imagine how helpless and alone she must have felt.

"I noticed the first spiderweb on the third day. There in the corner, across from my bed, way up high. To destroy it, I would need to climb a stool or stab at it with a broom. But of course I could do nothing of the sort. I was too weak to lift my hands, and could barely accept weak tea from a cup when the doctor and his nurse came to check on us."

At least there was a kind doctor. Like Titus, that might be the only reason she was still alive.

Her voice was shaky. "I didn't want to be there.

Not because of the spider, though I hated the creatures even then. My parents were in another room and I desperately wanted to be with them. They were too weak and ill for visitors, said the doctor. And I was too weak and ill to make visits. But that didn't stop me from wanting. I had nothing else to do, but lay there, minute after minute, hour after hour, one worried eye on the web across from me, yearning for the comfort of my parents."

His stomach twisted. He would never forget what it felt like to yearn for the comfort of his family. It was a wound that never healed.

She took a deep breath. "The next morning, there was a second web. Closer to my head this time. I tried to beg the nurse to destroy it, but she either couldn't hear me or did not understand the request. I'm not even certain actual sounds escaped my fever-parched lips. But I watched in panic as the webs grew ever larger."

Like the web of scars on the left half of his face. They brought him horror even today. He longed to brush them away. In his case, he deserved every mark. Miss Dodd, on the other hand, was blameless. She did not deserve any part of her tragedy.

Her face was still pale. "That afternoon, I woke up to the worst pain of my life. My toes had worked free from my blanket, and a spider had bitten me. My body reacts poorly to spider bites. Within minutes, my foot had swollen to twice its usual size. It was reddish purple and excruciatingly painful."

Pain on top of pain was something he understood all the way to his bones... and a misery he would not wish on anyone.

"The spider was still there, on my toe. I screamed. Or tried to. My swollen, hyper-sensitive skin could feel each of its spindly little legs tickling the pulsing bruise. I tried to kick it off and could not. I was terrified the foot would need to be amputated. Terrified the spider would bite the other leg as well, crawling up my body, biting and biting, until I was nothing more than a massive, swollen bruise."

It sounded like torture. No wonder she feared spiders. Their bites risked her life.

"Finally, the doctor and nurse returned to my bedchamber. Despite the alarming colors and elephantine condition of my swollen foot, their eyes were on mine, rather than my extremity. Whilst I was thrashing impotently against a monster smaller than a pea... My parents were in the next room, taking their final breaths. Dying without me, while my only care was for myself."

"That's not it at all," he said in horror. "You couldn't have known that was what was happening. Anyone would have been preoccupied with a bite reaction like that."

"It didn't feel that way," she said quietly. "They shared a sickroom, but I was isolated elsewhere, drowning in my loneliness, with all my focus on myself. It felt like I failed them. Abandoned them. I vowed that if I survived the bite and the fever, I would never be isolated or self-absorbed again. I'd keep my loved ones close. Be there for them, in life and in death."

Memories of his own family's last moments flooded Titus's mind. Memories he had tried so hard to keep buried.

Yet the parallels did not escape him. He was the only survivor of that long-ago accident that had left him physically scarred. Whereas she was the only survivor of a terrible fever and physically perfect. One wouldn't know anything unpleasant had ever happened to her by looking at her. One might even think she'd escaped unscathed.

"All I wanted was to say goodbye," she whispered, her voice breaking on the final syllable.

His heart went out to her. Her pain was evident. She was right. Just because the worst hours of her life weren't imprinted on her face for everyone to see did not mean that there were no wounds beneath the surface.

At least in her case, the deaths had not been her fault.

CHAPTER 12

*W*hen light and the noise of the street spilt through a break in the hedgerow ahead, Titus led the way toward the exit from the labyrinth with a mixture of dread and relief. He held no love for the dangerously crowded road just out-side the gardens, but Miss Dodd had been pale and jumpy ever since her encounter with the spiderweb, and he did not want her to continue to suffer.

"We'll be back at the hotel soon," he promised.

She flashed him a relieved smile, then frowned at the river of pedestrians streaming past the entrance of the labyrinth toward a different section of the botanical gardens. "Where is everyone going?"

Titus lifted his shoulders in a shrug. He neither knew nor cared what nonsense the merrymakers were up to. He hated crowds and would never take a bride, which made Marrywell's matchmaking activi-ties of no interest to him whatsoever.

Miss Dodd stopped in her tracks. "What time is it?"

He tugged the gold chain of his pocket watch up from his waistcoat and tilted the face toward her.

"We're late," she gasped.

"Late for what?"

"The tart-and-pie competition!"

Devil take it, Titus had forgotten all about the cursed tart-and-pie competition. "You still wish to attend?"

"I *must* do so." Her eyes were wide and beseeching. "It is my only opportunity to bid goodbye to Aunt Stapleton."

Goodbye. The thing she'd wanted to say to her parents, and had not been able.

Well, shite. There would be no talking Miss Dodd out of it. He glanced over her shoulder at Buttons, who hovered a discreet ten or twelve feet behind them, eyes lowered respectfully. As ordered, the maid stayed close enough to provide chaperonage, yet not so close as to interrupt her employer's conversation or activities.

Perhaps now Titus *wanted* her to interrupt. Perhaps he wanted Buttons to be the one to escort Miss Dodd to the damnable tart-and-pie competition, so that Titus needn't spend a single additional second in the torturous hustle and bustle of the surging Marrywell crowds.

But he couldn't abandon Miss Dodd. She'd been left alone too much already.

"Very well," he forced himself to say. "We'll go. Briefly. Long enough to say goodbye."

At least they needn't walk far. The tart-and-pie competition was held in the botanical gardens, just outside the entrance to the hedgerow labyrinth, on the same raised wooden dais where the May Day king and queen were crowned every year.

A long sideboard had been placed atop the dais, upon which stood several fresh, steaming trays. Behind each was the person who had baked the tarts and pies. Some chefs wore smug expressions. Others displayed almost comical nervousness.

That was, it might have been comical if Titus himself weren't actively trying to tamp down each of his own frayed nerves.

So many spectators filled the grass, it was worse than being on a dance floor. Shoulders banged into shoulders, elbows to elbows, hips to hips. He took a bonnet to the chin no less than three times before finally spying the tell-tale trio of ostrich feathers indicating Lady Stapleton's position in the melee.

He intended to drag Miss Dodd over there posthaste so that she could say her goodbyes and they could put this bloody festival behind them. But every step toward Lady Stapleton brought him within shouting distance of other Londoners who recognized him as the Earl of Gilbourne. Each tried to intercept his path so as to exchange a public greeting.

Titus hated small talk on a good day. Loud unsolicited greetings forced upon him so that the greeter could be seen conversing with an earl were even more offensive. He flexed his fingers and prepared to send them all to the devil, when—

"Do you really know all these people?" Miss Dodd asked in wonder.

He cut a sharp glance at her awed face. "No. I'm simply difficult to mistake for someone else."

But that wasn't the entire truth, was it? He did recognize a handful of the young bucks vying for his attention. Most were sons of the peers Titus worked with in the House of Lords. In fact… maybe they weren't angling for Titus's attention, after all. Perhaps it was the fresh-faced beauty at his side that had captivated them all at first sight.

The beauty he was supposed to be marrying off to a gentleman just like these.

With an aggrieved sigh, Titus forced himself to make the introductions between Miss Dodd and the various lords and dandies.

"Oh! Quite pleased to meet you!" she exclaimed every time, and somehow seemed to mean it.

Each of the fine gentlemen made a worse impression on Titus than the last. Their calculated compliments and grating chuckles and perfectly smooth faces. He wanted to fling them all away from Miss Dodd by smashing his fist into their patrician noses. But he locked his emotion inside and watched in cold, unfeeling detachment as she effortlessly charmed the whiskers off each new gentleman in turn.

It killed him inside.

Standing there in silence, giving tacit approval to each flowery flirtation... Damn it all, he should have stayed back at the tree and kept his eyes closed tight until the end of the week-long festival.

"My beautiful, delightful Miss Dodd," began a dandy as he bowed low over her hand, spangles swaying in the breeze.

Titus narrowly avoided tossing his beautiful, delightful Miss Dodd over his shoulder and stomping through the crowd. She wasn't the dandy's anything. For the next three weeks, she belonged to Titus. She was *his* ward, his—

His nothing. Titus did not own Miss Dodd, or her affections. He was supposed to actively be encouraging a match between her and literally anyone who wished to take her off his hands.

Hands that itched to reach for her and drag her away from this crowd, so Titus could once again have her to himself all over again.

But it wouldn't unfold like this. She didn't stare up at *him* with the same blushing cheeks, or giggle behind her gloved hand like she was doing at the inane attempts of poetry bubbling from the dandy's mouth like froth from a rabid dog.

Titus would never spout ridiculous romantic drivel. In part, because he looked every bit the monster on the outside as he was on the inside. Of course Miss Dodd wouldn't fawn at him like he'd hung the moon. He looked like the werewolf who howled beneath it.

"Ugh," came an openly disgusted female voice. "Of course you wouldn't have the good breeding to recognize none of us wanted to see *your* face here."

Titus turned, every muscle stiff, to see last year's diamond, Miss Bernice Charlton.

But she wasn't referring to Titus. Her sneer was aimed directly at Miss Dodd.

"*What,*" he growled, "did you just say to my ward?"

Miss Charlton sent him a startled glance as if just now noticing his presence—or recognizing the depths to which she had vexed him. She paled and clapped her mouth shut tight, as she should... Then she flummoxed him by fluttering her eyelashes and sinking into an absurdly obsequious curtsey.

"Why, Lord Gilbourne," she cooed in a voice that dripped honey. "Dare I hope you'll be at tonight's assembly? My dance card still has one space left."

Of all the potential responses to his outburst, this was the least expected.

"You told me *I* took the last spot," protested one of the young bucks nearby.

"If Lord Gilbourne wants it, then I'm afraid I must have forgotten to write your name down," Miss Charlton returned, with saccharine sweetness.

The dandy's face went red.

"*No*," Titus said coldly before things could get out of hand. "I shall not be at tonight's ball, or any future such event. Dance with whomever you please, but it will not be me."

Miss Charlton pouted. "You're the only one worth dancing with. I do hope you change your mind." She brushed the tip of her finger against his lapel.

He stiffened uncomfortably.

Miss Dodd slid between them at once, blocking Titus from Miss Charlton's grasp. "Rule number one: No touching."

Miss Charlton's laugh was the sharp tinkling sound of breaking glass. "Step aside, little orphaned ward. I'm certain you do not speak for the earl."

"And *you* ought not to speak at all, until you learn a modicum of respect," snapped Titus.

With that, he grabbed Miss Dodd about the waist and hauled her away from slack-jawed Miss Charlton and the rest of the shocked lords and dandies.

Rule number one bedamned.

CHAPTER 13

*L*ord Gilbourne's strong arm wrapped tight about Matilda as he steered them through the crowd like the prow of a pirate ship parting the sea. The revelers scattered from his path like droplets of water.

Rule number one: No touching...

Except when the earl was protecting her.

Matilda did not mind the possessive arm shielding her from the crowd. Lord Gilbourne's very presence was armor. Onlookers gaped shamelessly at him, rather than glance at Matilda. How she wished she could protect him right back! She'd toss every single person into the pond who treated his scars as fodder for their amusement and gossip.

The earl was stoic through it all, as always. Just as he never smiled, he also never looked sad or hurt or anxious. Anger seemed to be the only emotion he allowed himself to feel. Matilda could not make herself sorry that cruel Bernice Charlton had received the brunt of it for insulting her so openly.

Matilda *was* sorry that Lord Gilbourne was the only person who had taken exception to Miss Charlton's unflattering observations. Unlike Gilbourne,

Matilda suffered no shortage of emotions. The exchange had made her sad, and hurt, and anxious. And more than a little angry. At herself, for not fitting in. At the others, for not letting her.

She was also grateful, for the earl's unhesitating defense. Happy he was here. That he hadn't abandoned her, or concurred with the mocking comments.

Gilbourne would be appalled to hear this, but... At his core, the earl was *kind* and *nice* and *sweet*. He scowled to distract others from his scars. Or perhaps to enhance their impact, like a bear rising on its hind legs and flashing its enormous teeth. But behind all that was the real man. One whose first instinct was to protect, and to soothe, and to shelter.

She wanted to kiss him. Or hug him tight. Or both, repeatedly.

He did not release her from his side until they reached Aunt Stapleton. Only then did he drop his hand from Matilda's hip and fold his arms over his wide chest to scowl at them both.

"Make your goodbyes," he said coldly. "I cannot tolerate much more of this merriment."

"Oh, Titus," said Aunt Stapleton. "Do try to be reasonable. There are three more tarts yet to be judged."

Gilbourne's lips parted, no doubt to grind out a biting comment.

Before he could do so, Matilda rose on her toes so she could speak low into his ear. "I know you hate it here. Go back to the inn. Buttons and I will be safe with Aunt Stapleton."

Gilbourne looked as though he wished to argue— or rather, he looked like a reluctant guardian who thought he *ought* to argue—but desperately preferred the option of doing exactly as she'd suggested.

He gave a curt nod and matched her low tone. "Very well. Return straight after the competition. I'll have the carriages ready." He inclined his head toward Aunt Stapleton. "Stay well, godmother."

"And you, dear boy," Aunt Stapleton replied with obvious affection.

Gilbourne stalked off without another word.

"He means well," Matilda said quickly.

"No, he doesn't," Aunt Stapleton said with a fond chuckle. "Except to me, and apparently, also to you. I admit I am pleased to see the both of you getting on as well as I'd hoped when I devised this plan."

"He didn't want to be my guardian?" The reminder turned the warm feelings in Matilda's stomach into acid.

Aunt Stapleton's expression was kind. "He doesn't want to allow anyone at all into his life, much less past his defenses. A ward is good for him. He came to a *pie* competition."

"For five minutes," Matilda pointed out.

"Five more minutes than I'd ever dreamt," said Aunt Stapleton, shaking her head in wonder. "I wasn't the only one who couldn't believe my eyes. Everyone who recognized him was shocked to see him in public."

Was that it? Matilda wondered if Gilbourne had interpreted the stares as surprise at seeing a reclusive lord emerge from his cave, or if he believed they were simply gawping at the puckered ruin of his face.

She supposed both could be true at the same time.

"He never attends *any* public event?" she asked.

"No social events," Aunt Stapleton clarified. "He claims there's no point dancing with debutantes when he doesn't intend to take one as his bride. The truth is, he never leaves home at all, except to attend the House of Lords. Coming here to collect you is

86

probably the first time he's missed a session of Parliament since the day he first took his seat."

"He must resent me very much," Matilda said softly.

"You are the best thing that has happened to him. Like most people, Titus wishes to avoid embarrassment. What he fails to understand is that the answer is not avoiding life altogether. Nor is dedicating one's days to taking care of every citizen in England except for himself."

"He's involved in many initiatives?"

"He'd be chair of *every* committee, if they let him. My godson thinks that if he throws himself deeply enough into his duties to Parliament, it will fill up the emptiness inside. But human beings are social creatures. We all need other people. Including Titus, and including *you*, my dear."

"I'm trying to make friends," Matilda assured her great-aunt. "And I will do my best not to embarrass Lord Gilbourne."

"I know, darling. Anyone should count themselves fortunate to be your friend. It's time you step out of *your* nest and experience—" Aunt Stapleton winced as if a rocket had exploded overhead. She clapped both gloved hands to the sides of her head, cringing in obvious pain.

"Is it the megrim?" Matilda asked in dismay.

Her great-aunt had always suffered debilitating megrims, but could usually depend upon a month or two's reprieve between each agonizing attack. The most recent one had struck only a few weeks ago.

Aunt Stapleton squinted in obvious pain. "I'm sorry, love. I must return to my room at once and lie down in the dark with some laudanum if I'm to have any hope of traveling home tonight."

"I'll walk you there," Matilda said immediately.

87

"Don't be silly, you've only just arrived. You and Gilbourne stay and see who wins the competition. I'll expect a full recounting in a letter, as soon as you arrive in London."

Matilda and... Gilbourne?

Either her great-aunt hadn't heard Matilda whisper for the earl to return to the peace and quiet of his own room, or Aunt Stapleton had simply forgotten that small detail due to the severe pounding of her head.

Matilda certainly wasn't going to set her aunt straight now. She had no intention of quitting the festivities a moment sooner than absolutely necessary. Besides, Matilda had a chaperone, which made it all right. Buttons never trailed more than a few yards behind.

"If you're certain, Aunt." Matilda kept her voice low and calm, so as not to jar her aunt further. "I don't mind walking you to your room. I can rub your neck for you."

"No, darling, I'm certain," Aunt Stapleton said firmly. "Have a good time and make some friends. Try to talk Gilbourne into doing the same. I'll write to you as soon as I'm back in Shropshire."

"All right." Matilda's chest tightened. She gave her great-aunt a heartfelt hug. "Get some rest. I'll miss you."

"You'll be having too much fun to miss me or anyone." Aunt Stapleton patted Matilda on the back, then turned and hobbled off.

Matilda watched her go with a mixture of concern and elation. Aunt Stapleton's megrims could last for hours, or even days—but they always went away in the end. And Matilda was guardian-free for at least another hour. She was sorry the earl could not enjoy the festival, but Matilda had been having a splendid time—at least, until Bernice Charlton turned up and made such hateful comments. Now that Gilbourne had scared the young lady off, perhaps Matilda could finally set about making some friends.

She wasn't afraid of a challenge. She was New Matilda, the adventure-seeker. With luck, she would not only collect a bevy of new friends, but also pick up a few suitors in the process. Thereby proving to Gilbourne that she *could*. That it was essential for Matilda to attend social events. That she wouldn't embarrass him in the least.

She turned away from the dais with the tart-and-pie competitors and nearly smashed face-first into a gentleman's cravat. He was spindly and gray-haired and easily old enough to be her father, yet he looked at her as if being presented with a previously undiscovered treat.

"Where is your chaperone?" He licked his lips. "I simply must demand an introduction."

"Er," said Matilda, then gestured behind him. "My lady's maid is that way."

The lines on his forehead wrinkled further. "A lady's maid cannot perform introductions. Where's your mother?"

"Dead," Matilda answered. Perhaps being alone at the festival wasn't such a good idea after all.

"Now see here," said the older man. "There's no reason to get impertinent—"

A pretty young woman not much older than Matilda stepped between them. "Ah, Viscount Oldfield, there you are. I see you've met my good friend…" She raised an eyebrow at Matilda.

"Matilda Dodd," she whispered.

"Miss Matilda Dodd," continued the young lady smoothly, as if this introduction were the most normal thing in the world. "Miss Dodd was just telling me that she is family to…"

"Lady Stapleton," Matilda supplied.

"And that Miss Dodd herself is a resident of…"

"Rutland."

"Where she has lived since…"

"Birth. Twenty years ago. Almost twenty-one."

"Exactly so," said the young lady, as if all of this was old news. "Lord Oldfield's primary residence is in London, though he has a country home in Northumberland, where I am from." She dropped her voice so only Matilda could hear. "I, being Lady Tabitha Kerr. Pleased to meet you, old friend Matilda."

"The pleasure is mine, old friend Lady Tabitha," Matilda whispered back.

"You needn't horn in on my conversations," Viscount Oldfield said peevishly. "I won't tolerate such behavior now, nor after we're married."

Married?

Matilda gaped at Lady Tabitha, who made a face almost as pained as Aunt Stapleton with a megrim.

Lady Tabitha pointed over Viscount Oldfield's shoulder. "Is that Reuben Medford?"

"What?" The viscount turned around. "My nephew said he wouldn't be attending the festival this year. Where do you see him?"

"*Go*," Lady Tabitha mouthed, making shooing motions at Matilda. "Save yourself."

"Thank you," Matilda mouthed back, edging away from the viscount as quickly as she could whilst his back was still turned.

To think, a young woman like Lady Tabitha betrothed to a man of such advanced age! Who had shamelessly attempted to flirt with Matilda, despite being promised to another!

She sneaked a trio of diced peels from her reticule and popped them into her mouth.

All was not doom and gloom. She *did* make a friend today. Lady Tabitha seemed very sweet, and Matilda should not mind—

"*Ugh,*" groaned an all-too-familiar voice. "I thought I sent you back to your pen, little piglet."

CHAPTER 14

eeth grinding, Matilda turned to see Bernice Charlton smirking at her, whilst surrounded by four tittering magpies, all with identical ringlets and ivory fans.

Gilbourne's absence clearly had not escaped Miss Charlton's notice.

"Leave me alone," Matilda said, her voice shaking.

"Do us both a favor and stay home," Miss Charlton replied.

"Do all five of us a favor," said one of her porcelain cronies.

"Do the entire town the favor," said another.

The entire flock laughed mockingly.

"I'm not bothering you," Matilda gritted out.

"That cow pile of a gown is bothering all of us," Miss Charlton returned. "You're a blight on this beautiful festival. An eyesore for all of Marrywell. Gentlemen would run screaming rather than—"

"I was just talking to—"

"Viscount Oldfield?" Miss Charlton burst out laughing. "He would rut with a toad. No wonder he was interested in you."

"He tries to tup anything with a pulse," agreed one of her cronies.

"Pulse not required," added another.

"Although I might have thought he'd show better taste than... whatever *this* is." Miss Charlton made a derisive gesture toward Matilda's bodice. "Are you in costume as an impoverished milkmaid, or is that monstrosity truly the best your wardrobe has to offer?"

This monstrosity was not only one of Matilda's finest gowns, it had always been her favorite.

Until now.

Mortification clogged her throat, making it difficult to swallow. Blast Miss Charlton! Perhaps the very fact that this had *always* been Matilda's favorite gown indicated just how far out of fashion it had become. But was that any reason to tear someone down in front of an audience of thousands?

"Don't worry," she managed. "I'll be leaving soon. I'm off to London."

Miss Charlton burst out laughing. "Where you'll be shoveling horse manure with the street sweepers, dressed like that. No Town hostess would let an abysmal sight like you across her threshold."

Her words were needlessly, gleefully cruel, but... might Miss Charlton be right? Was Matilda already an embarrassment to Gilbourne, by her general appearance alone?

"Why do you care?" Matilda whispered, her throat thick.

"I care," Miss Charlton bit out coldly, "because you are standing in my way."

Matilda immediately stepped aside.

Miss Charlton rolled her eyes. "Don't be so literal, country lamb. I intend to marry your guardian, and I won't have you mucking up my plans. Stand back and let me have him. You'll soon learn I always get my way."

"And if you cross her..." one of her cronies said meaningfully.

"You'll live to regret it," warned another.

"Oh, I'm certain she already regrets being born," said Miss Charlton with a tinkling little laugh. "*I* certainly would if I were half as pathetic. Have you ever seen anything more embarrassing?"

The girls flounced off, cackling amongst themselves.

Matilda stared after them, her cheeks flushed with shame and her fingernails digging into her palms.

None of that had been necessary. Miss Charlton had been hurtful because she *wished* to be. To display her dominance and exert her superiority over... a piglet from the smallest shire in England. She swallowed hard.

Perhaps there *was* nothing Matilda could do to make people like her.

But she could at least try to blend in a little better.

She grabbed Buttons and dragged her out of the botanical gardens and onto the street.

"Back to the inn?" the lady's maid asked.

"No. I need to look less rustic," Matilda said in a rush. "Where's the closest modiste?"

Buttons' eyes widened. "I've no idea. I'm new to Marrywell."

"Someone has to know." Matilda stopped the next five passers-by, until she got her answer. Marrywell had exactly one seamstress fit for the upper classes. Matilda certainly wasn't a Lady Anything, but she needed to look the part. She couldn't keep making herself an easy target—or embarrass the earl. "Come on, Buttons."

They had to walk for over twenty minutes, then wait inside a well-appointed drawing room for over an hour, but eventually it was Matilda's turn to have an audience with Mademoiselle Henriot.

It took less than thirty seconds to ascertain that even if there was time to sew Matilda a gown before tonight's dancing—and there was not—at these prices, Matilda couldn't even afford a new bonnet.

"Please," Matilda begged. "I'll take whatever you have lying about. An old sample, anything."

"Child—"

"I'll pay double. I come into my inheritance in three weeks—"

"I'm to take your word?"

"Would you take the word of... the Earl of Gilbourne?" she blurted out.

The modiste didn't bother to hide her amusement. "Do you think I was born yesterday? Spare me your tall tales. Even the fanciest of courtesans cannot keep his attention for long. He's surely not trifling with *you*."

Matilda's face went bright red at the misunderstanding. "I'm not his mistress. I'm his— Oh, forget it."

Somehow, she stumbled out of the dressmaker's shop without bursting into tears. The sun did not make her feel better. Its brightness seemed to highlight everything that was wrong with her hair and shoes and gown. Everything that was wrong about *Matilda*.

"Back to the inn?" Buttons asked hesitantly.

"*Yes*," Matilda snapped, the word cracking in her throat and giving away her emotion. "You win. Everyone but me wins. I don't belong here."

They trudged back to the main road in single file,

Buttons refusing as usual to walk by Matilda's side, for propriety's sake.

Or perhaps because she, too, was mortified to be seen next to her.

When they arrived at the inn, there was no need to climb the stairs and enter the suite in search of Lord Gilbourne. He was standing in front of the hotel.

Wild-eyed and furious.

"Where the devil have you been?" he roared, grabbing her by the wrists. "When you didn't come back... I looked everywhere. Your aunt is in her room, and you had vanished completely."

"I..." Matilda's eyes stung, then she shook her head and lowered her gaze. "I'm sorry."

"Sorry? I could shake you for making me think something dreadful had happened to you. If you run away again, stay gone! I'm not chasing after you a second time."

"I didn't run away," she said in a small voice.

"Maybe you should have," he said harshly. "Perhaps if you'd succeeded at it, you would've done us both a favor—"

Matilda sucked in her breath at the unwelcome echo of Miss Charlton's vitriol. She wasn't going to cry. She *wasn't*. Even if she was every bit as much a bother and an embarrassment as Miss Charlton had intimated.

Gilbourne sighed and dropped her wrists. "If you didn't run off, then where did you go?"

Matilda didn't answer. She couldn't risk it. Every syllable threatened to spill out with a sob.

"To the modiste," Buttons piped up.

"The *modiste*?" Gilbourne repeated in disbelief. "In the middle of a tart-and-pie competition? Why the devil would she do that?"

"The other ladies were cruel to her," Buttons answered.

"Shut up, Buttons," Matilda mumbled. "You weren't standing close enough to hear."

"They called her a piglet and said she didn't belong," Buttons added.

"*Who* said that?" Gilbourne growled, his eyes flashing dangerously.

Matilda shook her head.

"Five of them," Buttons said helpfully. "They laughed at her in front of everyone. Others laughed, as well."

"That does it." Lord Gilbourne's fingers closed about Matilda's elbow. "Get into the carriage. We're going."

CHAPTER 15

*M*atilda supposed that any other rural born young woman desperate for change and adventure should be thrilled to find herself in a sumptuous carriage, barreling toward London.

And she *would* be. If there was the least hope of actually seeing any of it.

Her eternally scowling guardian sat at her side, scars facing away from her, his ankles crossed, arms folded, eyes closed, silent.

Matilda did not think for one moment that he had fallen asleep.

He was ignoring her. Occasionally Gilbourne's jaw would clench, or the muscle at his temple would twitch. Whatever he was thinking about so furiously vexed him to no end.

Probably Matilda.

Also possible: that she wasn't *that* important.

He might be cursing the journey that had pulled him from his comfortable seclusion and forced him, however briefly, into the public eye.

Or he might be thinking about all of the work he'd left unfinished in the name of duty. His responsibilities to the House of Lords. His hundred-and-one committees. His correspondence. His households, plural. Matilda did not know how many tasks the earl must manage. The only thing she knew for certain was that his responsibilities were legion, and she was one more item on a very long list.

She slid another of her slowly dwindling supply of tiny, candied peel bits into her mouth and watched him openly. She *ought* to be staring wide-eyed out of the window at the passing countryside and the myriad vistas she'd never before seen, but she could not tear her gaze away from her obviously disgruntled guardian.

Perhaps he could feel her watching him. Or perhaps he kept his eyes closed because he did not wish to look at *her*.

She wanted to grab his hand and to press his knuckles to her pounding chest and to assure him that she hadn't meant to embarrass him. Promise to never, ever embarrass him again.

But the truth was, she couldn't guarantee it. She was exactly what she looked like: a green country miss. His plan to tuck her away in a guest chamber for three weeks until she was no longer his problem… was undoubtedly the sanest, safest path for the earl.

If a frustrating one for Matilda.

Once she gained control of her inheritance, the sky would be the limit. She could do as she pleased, go where she wished. If only she knew where and what that was! She would wake up the morning of her twenty-first birthday a free woman, but without any notion how to navigate London. Or a single friend therein who wished to spend time with her.

How she'd hoped that Gilbourne…

She reached out her gloved hand and hovered it a

fraction of an inch above the earl's. She would not touch him—rule number one—but she could pretend he, too, wanted to grab her hand and comfort her. That he was seconds away from—

His pinkie finger twitched, bringing it in contact with Matilda's palm. She snatched her hand away, breathless. Even through their gloves, she'd felt a jolt of electricity. Or maybe the electrifying contact was nothing more than the carriage wheels bouncing over yet another rut in the road.

The earl's eyes opened, his piercing focus squarely on Matilda. "*What.*"

"W-what?" she echoed, stuttering. "Nothing. I… Nothing. Go back to sleep."

"I wasn't sleeping."

"Then resume thinking."

"*I* never cease thinking."

She smiled tightly and sucked on her candied lemon peel.

Of course she ought not to have run off to the modiste. Even if Matilda could have afforded the cost, the modiste was busy with dozens or hundreds of other clients and would not have been able to make a single stitch for Matilda until long after the festival was over. She understood that now.

In the moment, she'd simply yearned so hard to be accepted that she didn't let a little thing like logic stand in the way of potential friendship and happiness.

That her actions had worsened her already-strained relationship with her reluctant guardian was less than ideal. Of all the people Matilda wished might like her, Gilbourne was at the top of the list.

But her recent realization that sometimes there was nothing one could do to force someone else to want her presence in their life held true for the earl as well. Matilda could no more compel Gilbourne to accept her with open arms than she could win over Bernice Charlton and her entourage. Friendship was given voluntarily, or not at all.

No matter how much one longed for it.

Gilbourne was still scowling at her. "Who did it?"

She blinked. "Who did what?"

"Who made you run away?"

"I didn't run away. I was coming back. It was my idea. And a bad one. I apologize."

"What did they say to you that Buttons did not overhear?"

She shook her head, her cheeks flushing with shame at the memory. "No good can come of repeating it."

"Who insulted you? I want a list of names."

She crossed her own arms and glared back at him. Living through that indignity had been difficult enough. She would not relive it again. "One shouldn't speak ill of another."

"No," he ground out. "That's the dead. We don't speak ill of the *dead*. Rule number three: You speak as ill as possible about any living person who wrongs you."

"Why should I do so?"

"So that I can destroy them."

They glared at each other in silence, arms crossed, hips inches apart.

"You're making these rules up as we go along," she accused him.

He shrugged. "You must still comply. That's rule number two: What I say, you do."

She lifted her chin. "I'll fight my own battles."

He leaned forward, his voice low and full of portent. "Rule number four: Fight to win."

"I'll do that," she whispered, though it was a bluff.

The fight she most wanted to win was here in this carriage. The earl was close enough to hug. Close enough to kiss. If she leaned forward like he was doing...

He straightened. "Good."

Gilbourne turned his gaze toward the front of the carriage. A solid black wall. Even the panel to the driver was closed. The earl would rather look at nothing at all than at Matilda.

Her shoulders slumped back against the squab. "How long did you say the journey is?"

"Eight hours."

"Eight hours?"

"My coachman can manage it in seven and a half."

Of course he could. "How many hours have passed so far?"

"Three and a quarter." Gilbourne hadn't even needed to check his pocket watch to know the answer. Perhaps time was moving as interminably for him as it was for Matilda. "At least you are not atop a mail coach, Miss Dodd."

"I wasn't complaining about the carriage," she said quickly. "I've never been in a coach this fine *or* on a journey this long. And I told you: It's Matilda."

"Miss Dodd."

"Must we suffer so much formality? If I'm to call you Gilbourne, could you not call me... Dodd?"

The earl recoiled in horror. "Address you like a servant? You are not a maid, Miss Dodd. You are my ward."

"Then call me Tilly, as my parents did," she suggested.

His eyes glittered. "Let there be no confusion between us. I am not your father, Miss Dodd. I harbor no parental feelings toward you whatsoever."

She swallowed, then turned her gaze out the window. "Perhaps I'm just peckish."

Gilbourne rapped on the driver's panel at once. "John!"

The panel swung open and cold air rushed inside the coach. "Yes, my lord?"

"Stop at the first inn you find," Gilbourne ordered.

"There's one just ahead, my lord." The panel closed.

Within minutes, the carriage pulled into a traveler's inn. A row of carriages lined the front garden, and even more clumped before a large stable, where fresh horses could be rented and swapped.

"I thought you were in a hurry to return to your study," she stammered.

"I am," he said. "And you are hungry. So we eat."

"I'll hurry," she promised.

"Good. I hope to arrive before nightfall. There's an errand that... well, you'll see."

CHAPTER 16

They did not arrive before nightfall.

London stretched out on both sides of the carriage in a blur of black on black, with dazzling sparkles of yellow and white in the windows of the houses they passed. Matilda watched, transfixed.

Soon, the carriage pulled to a stop on a pretty little street lined with what appeared to be long rows of closed shops, with cozy residential lodgings above on the first and second floors. It was not at all what she had imagined for the Earl of Gilbourne's residence.

"Which one is yours?" she asked, unable to contain her eagerness to know this side of him.

"None of them," he replied flatly.

John Coachman swung the carriage door open.

Gilbourne stepped down from the coach, then turned and held his gloved hand up to Matilda. "Get out."

She scrambled up from the seat and hurried to place her hand in his.

"Fight to win," he reminded her.

"Is this a battlefield?"

"An armory. If Marrywell was a skirmish, London

104

is the war. The strategic advantage is that here, the combatants must follow certain rules—and I know every one."

"An armory?" she repeated in wonder. "Where are we?"

"Across the street from the most sought-after modiste in London. Madame Theroux's waitlist is two seasons long."

Matilda's mouth dropped open in excitement. "And we're on it?"

"No."

Her excitement fell and she frowned up at him with confusion. "We haven't two years to wait. We must find someone else."

"No one else will do. My ward shall have the best."

"But... you just said there's no possibility of her helping us."

"There's always a way." He dropped her hand and strode across the street, trusting that she would keep up.

There was no chance on earth Matilda would allow herself to be left behind. She all but glued herself to his side, matching each swift stride in perfect synchronicity.

A woman stood outside one of the many shops, locking a large wooden door between two enormous mullioned windows. Her other hand held a lantern. As they neared, Matilda could see extravagant gowns hung on display in each window.

Or perhaps these were ordinary walking gowns in London. The Earl of Gilbourne might know all the rules, but Matilda had never worn the uniform.

"Madame Theroux," came the earl's calm, authoritative voice. "I trust you have a moment to spare?"

The modiste turned around, her eyes widening upon sight of the earl's face. "Lord... Gilbourne?"

He inclined his head. "And my ward, Miss Dodd."

Matilda gave a little wave.

The modiste stared at her in open dismay, as if her chimney-sweep turned out more elegantly than Matilda currently presented.

Perhaps it was true.

"Lord Gilbourne," Madame Theroux said firmly, shaking her head. "With all due respect, your ward—"

"—needs an entirely new wardrobe," Gilbourne finished. "Yes. We're aware. That's why we've come to you. You're the best of the best, and the best is what we require."

"I haven't time for a project of this nature, my lord. My calendar is so full, I couldn't spare a moment to cut her a fresh ribbon for... *Mon dieu*, she's not even wearing a bonnet. Where on earth is her bonnet?"

"We need everything. Head to toe. The latest fashions."

"Milord, as I've just said—"

"Any price."

"Even if I charged you three times what I earn in an entire season—"

"*Any price*," he repeated. "And we'll tell everyone we've been on your list for five years, and that you are absolutely worth the wait. You know as well as I do that having my name attached to your creations will double or triple their value overnight."

She eyed him with avarice. "You'll say my work is so divine, every stitch is capable of entrancing even an infamously reclusive misanthrope like you?"

His jaw flexed. "It will be the first announcement I make to Parliament."

The modiste bit her lip, and gave Matilda another semi-despairing appraisal. "You said... any price?"

"Go with Madame Theroux," Gilbourne commanded Matilda. "She'll want to take measurements at once."

"Measurements at once," the modiste repeated, then fumbled her key back into the lock. "Come with me, Miss Dodd. We haven't a moment to waste."

When the door swung open, Gilbourne took the lantern from the modiste. "Wait here with Miss Dodd."

Madame Theroux frowned. "But you said—"

He edged her out of the doorway and strode inside the shop, disappearing into each room in turn. The glow from the lantern lifted high and sunk low, as if he were inspecting every inch of the wallpaper and floorings before allowing his ward inside.

He returned and handed back the lantern.

"What were you looking for?" asked a mystified Madame Theroux.

"Nothing." Gilbourne locked eyes with Matilda. "Go on in. It's safe."

Spiders. He had been sweeping for *spiders*.

"Thank you," she whispered. His thoughtfulness with her fears meant even more than his extravagance with the modiste.

"I'll wait in the carriage," he informed Madame Theroux. "When you finish, bring me my ward, and a number written upon a piece of paper. You'll have your bank deposit by morning."

"You're not coming with me?" Matilda blurted out.

He arched his brows. "To a dress fitting, in which you will be disrobed and measured? No, Miss Dodd. I will be in the carriage."

"I meant... Surely there's a waiting room..." she mumbled, her face aflame at yet another gauche mistake.

"Come along," Madame Theroux said briskly,

ERICA RIDLEY

pulling Matilda inside the shop and closing the door. "I'm missing my supper for this."

"It sounds as though you can now afford a bottle of champagne to go with your supper."

"A bottle? I'll soon be able to afford to install fountains of the stuff in every room. Lord Gilbourne has just cemented my career, and he knows it. That is, once I manage to turn you from..." She grimaced. "*this*..." A dismissive gesture accompanied the grimace. "...into the diamond of the ton."

"Diamonds are a good thing?" Matilda asked hesitantly.

"Diamonds are the *best* thing." Madame Theroux lit sconces in a small, pretty room and motioned for Matilda to turn around. "Miss Charlton *was* this year's diamond—and last year's, as well—which means it is time for a new queen to ascend to the throne, *n'est-ce pas?*"

"Miss... Bernice Charlton?" Matilda squeaked.

If Bernice had hated Matilda *before* her transformation...

But was it even possible to make a silk purse out of a sow's ear, as they say?

Madame Theroux could dress Matilda like a royal princess, but as soon as Matilda opened her mouth, everyone would know she was just... Matilda.

Her gown disappeared over her head, followed by her shift. Goosebumps flared across her flesh at the sudden exposure to the chill night air.

"Hold still," Madame Theroux commanded, her words muffled by the pencil clutched in her teeth. "Every stitch has to be perfect."

Matilda held herself as still as a post. She wanted adventure? Here it was. All she had to do was grab on tight. Her heart pounded.

Madame Theroux might be the fairy godmother

Matilda had been dreaming of. Her new wardrobe, the magic trick that caused all the frogs to turn into princes and fall in love on sight. Or at least, grant Matilda enough entrée to earn a few friends during her stay.

And if even this cosmetic transformation was not enough to keep the ridicule and loneliness away... Well, she would at least know she had tried as hard as possible.

"When Gilbourne said 'everything,'" Madame Theroux began, a coy note in her voice. "Did milord truly mean *everything?*"

"I have no idea what *you* mean," Matilda replied, baffled. "I don't know if he meant a walking dress or an evening gown or a riding habit or—"

"Oh, all of that and more, I'm sure. He did say 'from head to toe'. I'll assume he meant for me to include the full range of seductive undergarments to heighten nocturnal pleasures."

"The full range of... what?" gasped Matilda. "I— I'm his ward, not his wife."

Madame Theroux grinned with mischief. "What does that have to do with anything?"

CHAPTER 17

$\mathcal{B}$y the time Titus and his ward arrived outside his home, the sky was inky black and dotted with stars. None shone as bright as Miss Dodd, whose eyes sparkled in her radiant face.

She hadn't stopped smiling at him since emerging from the dressmaker's shop bubbling over with this new style or that, which Miss Dodd hadn't even known existed. Madame Theroux showed her fashion plates, and promised Miss Dodd she would soon look every inch as elegant and sophisticated.

"Thank you *so* much," Miss Dodd said for perhaps the hundredth time in five short miles.

"Stop thanking me," Titus growled. "And stop smiling."

She only smiled wider. He was glad for the darkness cloaking them. Even in the shadows, her beauty was almost too bright to bear.

John Coachman opened the carriage door. As before, Titus banished him with a look, so that Titus should be the one to hand Miss Dodd out of the coach and onto the starlit street.

"This is Mayfair?" Her head swiveled in all directions, eyes wide—and surprised. "I understood it to be full of terraced homes; enormous brick buildings divided amongst multiple families."

"This is not Mayfair," he replied. "Too crowded and too many carriages. I live on the edge of London on a large plot of land so that I needn't look at other people."

"And because it's beautiful," she guessed. "So many trees and flowers! Your home is lovely to look at from the outside, even at night. All the candles in the windows! I imagine each of those windows come morning offers a breathtaking view surrounded by nature."

"What I value most is peace and quiet," Titus said repressively.

An ambiance that was soon to be in short supply, if the past few days with the talkative, sunny Miss Dodd were any indication.

On the outbound journey to Marrywell, he had been resentful of the intrusion of a ward, and the disruption to his meticulously ordered life. After spending time with her, Miss Dodd's presence still wasn't convenient... but he found himself looking forward to each new glimpse of that infectious smile.

The visit to the modiste had little to do with his role as guardian, and was only partially spurred by the poor treatment Miss Dodd had received from Titus's peers. Even if she should never see those people again—and God knew, Titus had no desire to go anywhere there might be people—every penny of the expense had been well worth the pure delight a new wardrobe had brought to her face.

When the butler, Kelly, opened the door to receive his employer, Titus ushered Miss Dodd into the receiving area. Seconds later, Buttons arrived from the second carriage, along with a pair of footmen bringing in the valises.

"I'll take Miss to her room to get settled," Buttons chirped, obviously over the moon at being able to put her skills to use.

"One moment. Wait here," Titus commanded.

He brushed past the women and into the corridor, where his housekeeper, Mrs. Harris, was hurrying to greet him.

Titus kept his voice low. "Please ensure that there are no spiderwebs in the house, particularly not in any room my ward might conceivably enter."

Mrs. Harris did not hide her offense. "Of course there are no spiderwebs in this home, my lord! You will never encounter so much as a speck of dust on any surface. The day you encounter—"

"No. You do not understand. If a spider enters this home whilst Miss Dodd is under my protection, I will sack every member of this staff."

The housekeeper's eyes widened. "Oh. She—"

"No one is even to say the word in front of her, or allude to spiders or webs in any manner. Am I clear?"

"As glass." Mrs. Harris nodded briskly. "It shall be as you desire."

He arched his brows when she did not run off at top speed.

She blanched. "Straight away."

"Thank you." After his housekeeper hurried to warn the others, Titus strode back into the receiving area. He flicked his wrist at Buttons. "Take her upstairs and do your job. I don't want to see either of you again until I've slept and breakfasted."

"I'm standing right here," said Miss Dodd.

"Then I needn't repeat myself," he said coldly.

Rather than appear chastened, she wished him a cheerful good night before disappearing up the stairs with her lady's maid.

Titus didn't realize he stood there in silence,

watching her go, until the butler's voice nearly startled him out of his boots.

"She seems truly lovely," Kelly commented.

"She'll be gone in three weeks," Titus snapped. "I cannot wait for the return to normalcy."

He strode off before the butler could respond. Titus did so more out of self-preservation than a desire for rudeness. Kelly was an observant old goat. Titus had no wish to know what, precisely, might have been observable on his face as he gazed after Miss Dodd.

The earl had a plan. He always had a plan. And this one was simple: Never allow her under his skin. The most important lesson he'd ever learnt was that if you refused to let yourself care about someone, then losing them could not hurt.

Titus would not care about his ward. He was looking forward to her imminent departure.

If he was grumpier than usual, well, it must be due to her disruptive presence and not the prospect of renewed peace and solitude in three weeks' time.

CHAPTER 18

*T*itus awoke mid-morning, more determined than ever to concentrate on ignoring the new presence in his household. Pretending they were not living together now, would make the transition all the easier once they separated for good.

In fact, the wedge he did his best to drive between them was more for Miss Dodd's benefit than his own. Titus was the worst person with which to co-habitate. Ha. An understatement. Others would be wise not to allow him into their lives at all.

People like his little brother, whose thinning and yellowed baby blanket Titus woke up every morning with his face pressed deeply into, as though the aged and fraying material still held any trace of Oliver's long disappeared scent.

Foolish, illogical self-indulgence. Titus flung the blanket from his bed in disgust. Another traditional part of his morning routine.

He swung his legs over the side of the bed and propped his elbows on his knees, burying his face in his hands. *Burying.* Apt. Every time he closed his eyes, he remembered that tiny coffin… and his starring role in the tragedy. After suffering less than a minute of Titus being Titus, all three of his family members lay crumpled and lifeless. He was destructive. Toxic. And he had no business seeking any comfort from his long-dead brother.

Titus launched himself out of bed. He scooped up the limp square of linen, rending it into a dozen jagged pieces with a mighty roar. There. The tie was severed at last. He had never deserved a connection to begin with. Had never merited the affection of anyone foolish enough to bestow any upon him.

Without the blanket to give him a false sense of forgiveness—

The door swung open and the earl's valet Augustin rushed into the bedchamber. "My lord, are you all right? I heard an awful noise."

Awful. That was Titus. Without turning around, he swiped his palm surreptitiously over his cheeks then stared down at the ruined scraps littering the floor by his feet.

"It's nothing." His swollen throat was almost too tight to force the words out. "Gather up these rags and burn them."

"Burn them?" Augustin crept forward hesitantly, then sank to his knees to gather up the last remaining pieces of Titus's baby brother. "I am certain that Mrs. Harris or one of the maids could—"

"*Burn them.*" Titus's fists dug into his sides as his stomach churned. "Then leave me in peace. I'll dress myself. I've no need of your services today, and if you ever question an order again, I shan't see any need for your continued services in the future."

"Yes, my lord. Understood." Augustin scrambled to his feet and backed out of the room, bowing and scraping as he went.

Titus didn't look up from the floor until the door shut tight and he was alone once again.

His muscles did not relax. The opposite. He felt worse than ever. It took every ounce of his iron will not to chase after Augustin, knock his valet to the ground, and snatch back every single scrap that had once belonged to Oliver.

Stiffly, Titus set about shaving half of his face— the scarred side saved him that much effort, at least —and dressing in the clothes Augustin had ironed and set out for him the night before. His valet had done so without consulting his employer's preferences. Titus had made it clear on Augustin's first day, that the earl didn't give a fig about the garments he put on his body. Titus didn't care to impress others, or even to leave the privacy of his study.

But today... after last night... He could not help but wonder whether his attire lived up to Miss Dodd's innocent expectations of a respectable society gentleman. Or if his disinterest in following fashions marked him as every bit the outsider those sanctimonious prigs had accused her of being.

No matter. Titus wasn't going to replace his wardrobe, even if it lagged far behind *la mode du jour*. This was who and what he was. And he wasn't trying to impress Miss Dodd. There was no point. She would soon be gone from his life, leaving no more evidence of her presence behind than the ashes from Oliver's blanket. So be it.

Once he was clean and dressed, Titus retrieved the novel from his nightstand and made his way down the stairs to the breakfast table, where he would spend an hour turning the pages of his book with one hand whilst half-heartedly picking at a plate of cold toast with the other, as he did every morning.

Except, *this* morning, he arrived to discover more than cold toast in the breakfast room. Miss Dodd was already seated at the table, a plate piled with eggs and kippers and fresh buns before her.

At his arrival, she flashed a guilty look from beneath her lashes. "I'm sorry I didn't wait for you. I wasn't certain when you would rise, and Cook had assured me it should be no bother at all for the menu to include—"

"Stop. Talking." He tossed his book next to his empty plate and dropped heavily into his chair, leaning forward to rub his temples.

"You sound horrid. Have you a megrim?" Miss Dodd sprang up from her chair, abandoning her breakfast, dashing behind Titus's chair in a flash. "I know just the thing to… Oh. I forgot." Her voice trailed off hesitantly. "No touching."

He held himself stiffer than ever, his fingertips frozen at his temples, his nostrils twitching from the warm fresh clean scent of her enveloping him from behind.

"Do whatever you please," he growled. "Then eat your breakfast."

There was a pause, and then her hands settled at the base of his neck and over the ridge of his shoulders. Slowly, firmly, her thumbs kneaded the tight tendons and rigid muscles. Though her hands never strayed from the base of his neck and the top of his shoulders, Titus's muscles grew limp. His hands fell from his temples to dangle loosely at his sides. Even his throat was no longer clogged. It was as though each stroke mended a tiny thread over the holes he had ripped in himself when he'd destroyed his brother's blanket.

"Is it helping?" she asked, her voice soft and soothing.

"I don't know what one's neck and shoulders should have to do with a headache," he said coldly.

117

"You'd be surprised how many headaches are contained in one's neck and shoulders. Shall I continue a little while more?"

He never wanted her to stop. "Go and eat your breakfast. You've done enough."

Miss Dodd retook her seat without the least sign of offense or chastisement. She dove back into her eggs as though no interruption whatsoever had occurred.

Just in time. The door to the dining room swung open and Cook strode through, wiping her hands on a flour-dusted red apron. "What did you think of the tarts, Mattie? If you prefer elderberry to fig, I can always…" Her round face paled at the sight of Titus. "My lord! Good morning! Your toast has been waiting since dawn, as you requested."

His voice was a dangerous growl. "*What* did you just call Miss Dodd?"

"Oh, I asked her to," his ward said breezily. "Anyone who beats me at Loo and Commerce deserves to first-name me. Which essentially puts me on equal footing with every member of your household. Or unequal footing, depending on how you view it. By my count, it was only the ten-year-old hall boy who failed to annihilate me at least once during—"

"You played cards with my servants?"

"Not for money," she said quickly. "Rhoda has a jar of pretty pebbles she collected from the river, which serve perfectly as game currency. No need for fancy ivory fish like Aunt Stapleton carries. Although if we *had* played for money, George and Isaiah might not have shown up for work today and taken an extended holiday instead. I don't think I've ever lost that much at one sitting, except for the time—"

"Who the devil are George and Isaiah and Rhoda?" he burst out.

"Stable-master, footman, and chambermaid," Cook murmured. "You know them as John Coachman, John Footman, and—"

Oh, enough! "Miss Dodd, I forbid you from fraternizing with servants."

"You can't. Or rather, you can forbid all you like, but I've already given my word to join in on the nightly games whenever I am home to enjoy them."

"This is not your home," he sputtered, then glared at Cook. "You all play nightly games? Do I not assign enough tasks to—"

"Oh, don't be such an ogre," said Miss Dodd with an indulgent wave of her hand, then smiled conspiratorially at Cook. "Is he always like this before his morning toast?"

Cook wisely refrained from opining, and fled to the safety of the kitchens instead.

Unconcerned, Miss Dodd resumed her breakfast.

Titus dropped three pieces of hard toast onto his plate. He made a production of placing his book right in front of his face and removing its crimson ribbon.

Miss Dodd continued eating.

He turned his head away from her and concentrated all of his focus on the written word, doing his best to lose himself into a tale of heroics and adventure as he did every morning, whilst knowing his ward would interrupt him at any moment.

She did not.

Was she even still here? The sounds of eating had ceased. Had she left the breakfast room?

Titus waded through one more chapter before turning his head just enough so that he could peek out over the top of his book at her from the corner of his eye.

Miss Dodd was reading her *own* book.

He stared crossly at her, heroic adventures forgotten. How dare she... copy him companionably... by bringing her own reading material unrequested... and doing nothing to disturb his peace and quiet.

It galled him to admit that if Miss Dodd was intolerably distracting, it was not because of any disruptive action she had taken, but rather Titus's own inability to look at anyone else or think of anything else when in her presence. Heaven help him.

If she was captivating now... The new wardrobe was going to be an absolute disaster.

CHAPTER 19

fter breakfast, Titus had intended to remove to his study and resume all of the preparations and correspondence for the committee projects he'd had to put on hold whilst he was off in Marrywell. He took his novel to his library instead. He'd read three chapters at breakfast—or tried to; he'd turned the pages anyway—and resolved to begin the segment anew, this time with his full concentration.

Miss Dodd followed him into the library with her own book and settled wordlessly in the chaise opposite.

He glowered at her.

She licked her lips and turned a page.

He watched her in growing aggravation as she apparently experienced no hindrance whatsoever to losing herself in her own novel. She did not display the slightest hint of distraction due to the scowling earl with a white-knuckled grip on his own book three feet away.

Titus wanted to ask what she was reading that was so bloody enthralling, but heroically refrained. Nothing made him more homicidal than whenever a passer-by interrupted him mid-climactic scene to ask, *Having a nice read?* or to comment, *Good book, is it?*

And yet there was no hope of him returning to his fictional adventure when his very real ward was seated an arm's width away.

He settled on increasing his glowering.

She continued reading, oblivious, as the seconds turned into minutes and the minutes turned into half an hour. At last, she made a happy little sigh and closed her book. When she glanced up, she appeared startled to discover him still in the library, right in front of her.

"Oh!" She hugged her novel to her chest. "Did you finish yours, as well?"

"No, I did not," he bit out sourly, and tossed his book aside. "I suppose now that you've nothing constructive with which to entertain yourself, you'll wish to go out on the town and see a bit of London."

She tilted her head as though his words made no sense. "You hate London. You'd rather sink to the bottom of the sea than ferry a tourist about from sight to sight."

"I don't hate London," he groused. "And I never offered to accompany you on such an insipid outing."

"You would never send me off alone," she said with confidence. "And I would never ask you to make yourself miserable on my behalf. This book belonged to my aunt, so I'll have to return it, but I see you have many others. If you don't mind me borrowing one, I'm happy to stay indoors and read with you."

"Stop being so deuced..." *Reasonable.* Likable. Sweet.

She waited patiently, eyebrows up, lips parted in polite interest.

He huffed and rose to his feet. "Get your pelisse on, then. I refuse to go near Vauxhall, Hyde Park, the shopping districts, or anywhere crowds and traffic might form, but I suppose we could take a short walk in one of the less frequented parks whilst everyone else is still abed."

Her eyes brightened and she set her book aside at once. "I would adore that. Thank you."

"Don't expect me to take you anywhere else," he warned her, as he led her down the corridor toward the front door. "I'm very busy, and even if I weren't, I wouldn't be caught dead at some fashionable crush. My man of business has been instructed to file all invitations directly into the closest fire."

"I understand," she promised.

Titus summoned Buttons to accompany them as chaperone. The lady's maid did not bother to hide her delight.

Miss Dodd accepted her pelisse from the butler and allowed Titus to hand her into the carriage. "Would it be easier to host small, intimate gatherings yourself in order to control their size and nature, rather than attend someone else's soirée?"

He shuddered. "I should rather lock myself in my own valise than host a party of any number."

She nodded thoughtfully, though he glimpsed what might have been the briefest flash of disappointment flicker in her eyes.

Damn it all, he did feel like an ogre. He hated society gatherings, but she clearly did not. Rather, Miss Dodd didn't know if she enjoyed such events, because she was from a village smaller than his shoe. By refusing to escort her to any of London's most celebrated entertainments, Titus was being grossly unfair to his ward.

He locked his jaw in disgust. Oh, very well. He would have his man of business write back to all the hosts whose correspondence met a fiery demise. He'd request replacement invitations to anything occurring in the next three weeks, and would specify Miss Dodd's explicit inclusion if they wished the reclusive Earl of Gilbourne to consider attending.

They would all comply. His attendance would be a coup for any hostess, largely because he was unwed and wealthy—a horrific combination when trying to avoid entanglements of any kind. Debutantes and the desperate alike were willing to look beyond both surliness and scars if there was gold or a title in their future.

The carriage drew to a stop.

Miss Dodd peered in all directions as he handed her down. "Where are we?"

"Green Park," Titus replied. "It's the worst of the royal parks. No lake, no follies, no fashionable promenade. Forty-seven acres of plain green nature. At this hour, nobody fashionable is out of bed, much less having a promenade. There will be no one to converse with."

"Besides each other," she said with a happy smile. "If you love it, then so shall I."

He gave her his elbow rather than respond. It was a horrifically beautiful day, which likely meant that his luck would not, in fact, hold, and their stroll would be beset upon by any number of other pedestrians.

For the first time, however, other people were not Titus's primary concern. As they walked, he found himself scanning every inch of the path for tell-tale gossamer webs.

If this new preoccupation was disconcerting for him, he could not imagine how difficult it must be for Miss Dodd, who lived every moment of her entire life in fear of a spider springing out from nowhere. It was a wonder she was willing to go out into the world at all.

He was glad that at least for the moment, she needn't do so all alone.

CHAPTER 20

$\mathcal{T}$itus *tried* to enjoy the nature blooming around them, truly he did. Before becoming the sort of man who rarely left the four walls of his study, he had once been the sort of lad to run wild across fields of grass, pick flowers for his mother, climb trees with his brother, and spot birds with his father.

His description of Green Park to Miss Dodd may have been less than generous, but the truth was, Titus had always been happiest when surrounded by green spaces. The cool breezes and the fresh scents and the rustling leaves filled him with a peaceful calm he could not replicate anywhere else.

That had all been true… until now.

Today, his heart was anything but calm. He hadn't spotted a single bird, because he was physiologically unable to tear his sidelong gaze from Miss Dodd. Every flower they passed, he wanted to snatch up for her. As for climbing trees—he had a suspicion she would enjoy that activity even more than receiving flowers.

He settled for scowling instead. If he could not control his reaction to her presence, at least he could dissuade her from glancing in his direction or attempting friendly conversation.

It didn't work.

"What a lovely day," she said with a happy sigh. "The park, the company, the soft warmth of the morning sun... No wonder the beau monde visit the royal parks all the time."

She enjoyed the company? He shot her a skeptical look out of the corner of his eye.

"The ton don't visit the parks. They visit Hyde Park. Not in the mornings, or every day, but from two to five in the afternoon on Sundays, as if reporting to a post for duty. And only during the season. They haven't the least idea what the park itself looks like. The point of the drive and the promenade is to be seen by each other."

She glanced up at him with curiosity, her hand still curved about his elbow. "How do you know so much about what the beau monde does and doesn't do, if you don't take part?"

"I grew up among them," he reminded her. "I have been coached in proper behavior and the habits of the haut ton since I was old enough to toddle. Besides, their activities are printed in the morning paper as though their antics were as newsworthy as the war with Napoleon or the exchequer bills."

She blinked. "Exchequer?"

"One of my committees," he muttered. Why on earth was he even talking about this? He was becoming as loquacious as his ward. "Never mind. It's not important."

"It sounds like it's *very* important. More important than the lords and ladies of polite society. I would like to visit the House of Lords and hear more about what truly matters."

"Well, you can't. Only men are allowed in the visitors' gallery inside the main chamber. Which is dreadful anyway. Rows of long wooden benches stuffed with men in tailcoats and top hats, sweating and pontificating for hours."

"Women can't even listen?"

"There are small ventilation apertures in the attic where the smoke from the chandeliers escapes. Some women do peer down from there. Less crowded, but even worse smells and temperature. And no bench upon which to sit. Just a hole to poke one's head through awkwardly."

Rather than be repulsed by this description, Miss Dodd's eyes shone. "It sounds like an unforgettable experience. Will you take me, the next time you attend Parliament, so that I can watch you give your speeches on important matters?"

"No," he said flatly.

"Will you give your speeches to me privately, so that I might be more informed that way?"

"No," he said again. His heart gave a little pang at the cozy domestic image. Miss Dodd would be exactly the sort of female who would not only listen with rapt attention, but also have unexpected insights of her own.

As good an idea as it was, there was no sense starting something that would not continue. He shouldn't even be here in the park with her. Buttons was chaperone enough for a young lady. Titus knew better than to get used to someone he was destined to lose.

Miss Dodd did not appear deflated by his reaction. "We didn't receive the London papers out in Rutland where I grew up. While I'm here, I'll read every word, and educate myself on the ways of the beau monde as well as the important political issues of our day."

Titus could not think of a good reason to forbid this plan. True, ladies were not supposed to have vocal political opinions. But a well-informed bride would be Miss Dodd's future husband's problem, not Titus's.

Then again, he was supposed to be marrying her off. His godmother had specifically exhorted him to ensure his ward made the best match possible. His jaw tightened.

So far, all Titus had done was keep her to himself. A miser hoarding his treasure.

"Look!" Miss Dodd pointed up ahead with excitement. "Other people are here on our path."

"Don't point," he snapped. "It's rude."

His ire was not with his ward, but with the identity of the three individuals she had spotted. Handsome younger sons of well-respected lords. Any one of them should make an enviable match for Miss Dodd.

"Do you know them?" she whispered.

"Yes." Which meant when their paths crossed, they would greet Titus by name... and wait expectantly for the earl to introduce the beauty at his side.

A task he would then be obligated to perform. No matter how he felt about it.

The trio were upon them in no time. Titus had no doubt they'd glimpsed his ward's attractive silhouette and picked up their pace before Titus could come across a convenient fork in the path to whisk his ward away.

"Good morning, Lord Gilbourne," the men murmured politely, their gazes not on Titus but on Miss Dodd. "How do you do this fine day?"

Miserable. As usual.

He gritted his teeth a few seconds more, just to

make them squirm, then made the expected introductions.

All three men were the picture of friendly flattery, but to Titus's surprise, Miss Dodd reacted not by responding flirtatiously in kind, but by retreating into uncharacteristic silence. At each flirtatious word from the young lords, she closed up more and more, like a flower being deprived of sunlight.

"We must go," Titus interrupted. "We're late. Good day."

He made an about-face that would have been unforgivably rude if he hadn't offered his curt explanation—and was still abominably discourteous all the same.

But he didn't care about the lords and their precious feelings. There would be other ladies to flirt with. Other women to court.

All Titus cared about was Miss Dodd.

CHAPTER 21

$\mathcal{T}$itus waited until they were tucked back into the safety of his home before demanding to know how the lords had offended Miss Dodd, so that Titus could put a stop to it.

Her eyes widened. "No, no. It wasn't them. It was me."

He frowned. "You?"

She cast her gaze about the library in obvious distress, then shook her head. "It's too mortifying."

Titus glanced over her shoulder. "Buttons. Out. Close the door behind you."

The maid paled. "But propriety dictates—"

"*Out.* If I have to say it a third time, you'll be out on the street."

Buttons scurried from the library with alacrity, shutting the door firmly behind her.

"There." Titus turned back to Miss Dodd. "Now you will tell me the problem, and I shall resolve it."

Her cheeks flushed. "It's just... I thought I was ready. When Aunt Stapleton said we'd be going to Marrywell, it sounded like a grand adventure. I would meet fine lords and ladies. I would dance at a ball."

"And I took you away before you could take a single step."

"No one was going to ask. I'd failed to account for the fact that *I* am not a fine lady, but a country bumpkin. I don't look the part or act the part or have any part at all."

"You'll look the part soon enough. Madame Theroux will deliver each item as she finishes it."

"Then I will be an oinking piglet in French fashions."

"I have not noticed any such lapse in decorum."

"That is because you are a sweet man with a kind soul."

Titus stared at her, speechless. Literally no one had ever described him in such a shockingly inaccurate manner. Not as a child, and certainly not as a grown man.

"The others…" Miss Dodd bit her lip. "If I were to attend a ball, they'd laugh at me. I wouldn't know what to say or how to act to fit in."

"Trust me," said Titus. "The most piercing question you'll be asked is for your opinion on the weather. Whilst dancing, you needn't talk at all if you'd…" He narrowed his eyes. "Can you dance?"

"Yes, of course. Well, somewhat. That is, I can in theory."

"What the devil does *that* mean?"

"It means my parents taught me. I never had a proper tutor, or any public occasion in which to practice. I've taken several turns about my parlor… which, I must confess, did not much resemble what I saw in that ballroom. I can muddle through the pattern of a quadrille, but I haven't the least notion how to waltz."

"You can't waltz," he repeated.

She shook her head.

He let out a long suffering sigh. "Come here."

A frown marred her forehead. "Pardon me?"

"I said, come here." He shoved the chairs out of the way, then pulled her to him, lifting her right hand shoulder-high and settling his other palm on her left hip. "If those nodcocks can do it, so can you. Follow my lead."

He hummed a slow French waltz under his breath as he led her into the steps.

Her feet stumbled at first, then quickly caught on to the rhythm. By the second loop about the library, her movements were as graceful as any Titus had ever encountered. Miss Dodd would not embarrass herself on the dance floor.

She would enchant the hearts of every man who danced with her, instead.

His chest tightened and he glared down at Miss Dodd.

She smiled up at him. "You have a lovely singing voice."

He ceased humming abruptly, though he did not yet relinquish her from his arms. He was not certain that he could stop waltzing with her.

"Do you hate this?" she asked, her voice hesitant. "Dancing?"

He adored it. Had always loved moving his body, and especially enjoyed the sensation of her ungloved hand in his. The feel of her soft curves beneath his fingers.

"Waltzing is… tolerable," he admitted begrudgingly. "With you."

The smile that blossomed on her face filled his entire body with sunshine. One needn't visit a park for fresh air when one held Miss Dodd in one's arms. She was the song of every bird, the smell of every flower, the caress of every breeze.

Worse, when she looked at him like this, he found himself more and more actively trying his hardest not to return her contagious smiles.

He, who had not smiled in well over a decade! Trying *not* to. And very nearly failing in the endeavor.

"Thank you," she said softly.

He pulled her a little closer as they waltzed. The library was too small to do the dance justice, but Titus didn't care about anything outside of the woman in his arms. The enclosed circle of their embrace had become his entire world. Her warmth, a comfort. Her softness, incredible. Her lips, irresistible.

He forced his gaze away from her mouth and up to her eyes. She was staring at him as though he'd transformed into a handsome prince.

Titus knew better, of course. His face was the stuff of nightmares, and his manners not much better. He was not the hero of the fairy tale, but the beast to be slain so that the beautiful princess could live happily ever after.

But he could not let her go. Or look away. *Her* face was nothing short of that of an angel. She didn't need ball gowns and French fashions to hold his heart in her hands. She just had to look up at him like she was at this moment. Eyelashes heavy. Lips parted. As though longing for his kiss.

He willed himself to keep his heart hardened and his walls strong. He would not, *could not*, allow himself to feel more for her than any other duty he was responsible for as an earl. Keeping every semblance of emotion locked away was the only way to ensure he would not care when she inevitably vanished from his life and he found himself once again all alone.

"You know," she said with a sweet smile, "you could first-name me if you wished to."

"I don't wish to."

"But if you did, you could call me Matilda."

"I thought I said waltzes were to be performed in silence."

"You said one needn't feel *obliged* to converse. I don't feel obligated to talk to you. I enjoy it."

He glared down at her. What the devil was he supposed to say to that?

"'Thank you, Mattie,'" she parroted in a deep voice. "'I am fond of talking to you, too. You are my favorite ward.'"

"*Stop*," he commanded before the smile lurking behind his sneer managed to break free. "I'm not fond of anything, least of all the inconvenience of a ward."

"'Which is why I took you to the dressmaker, Tilly,'" she continued in her faux-deep voice. "'And enjoyed a private stroll with you in the park. And then banished your maid in order to pull you scandalously close for a waltz.'"

It did not quite sound as coldhearted and cruel as Titus prided himself on portraying.

"I am merely imitating the sort of interaction a young lady might find herself in at a ball," he informed her. "You would do well to curb your impertinent tongue. An unscrupulous rake will do whatever he must to shut you up."

Her eyebrows shot skyward in challenge. "Would he? I find myself positively quaking in my dancing slippers to discover what dastardly behavior a rake might employ. Show me."

His jaw hardened. "If anyone flirts inappropriately or even *pretends* he might steal a kiss, you are to slap him and scream for help."

She wiggled her fingers against his upper arm. "Slapping hand ready. Show me what I am to avoid at all costs."

This was a terrible idea.

"Stop me before I make contact," he warned her. "This is all pretend."

"'Stop me, my darling Tilda,'" she corrected him in her mocking earl voice. "'Stop me, my fair Mattie-Mat-Mat.' 'Stop me, my sweet, mellifluous—'"

He kissed her.

She didn't slap him.

Their mouths locked together as if designed by a master clockmaker never to part.

The waltz vanished. Her arms wrapped tight about his neck. His own wound about her waist, hauling her so close that every soft curve of her body pressed flush against every hard plane of his.

Inappropriate behavior. Scandalous behavior. Rakish behavior.

He could not stop. She tasted of sugar and citrus, sweet and refreshing. Her curves were heaven, and her embrace... When was the last time Titus had been embraced? He knew the exact date. The last warm hug he'd received had been the morning of the fateful crash. Ever since that day, few could bear to look straight at him, much less touch him. Many courtesans could not even hide their revulsion.

But Miss Dodd—Titus's fair, mellifluous Mattie-Mat-Mat—somehow looked at her beast of a guardian and saw a man she wanted *closer*. A man she was glad to touch. A man she was eager to kiss.

And Titus... Good God, how was he supposed to defend himself against that?

He could try as much as he liked to keep her at arm's length, but such effort was patently in vain. She'd ceased staying at a safe distance days ago.

Miss Dodd wasn't attempting to breach his defensive walls. She was already holed down in the trenches *with* him. Snuggled close, with her hand held tight in his.

And as for teaching her a lesson...

It was Titus who was learning he was very much in far over his head.

CHAPTER 22

*M*atilda wrapped her arms about Gilbourne's neck and kissed him for all she was worth. Not that she needed to hold on tight. He was holding on tight enough for both of them. She was up on her toes for politeness' sake, but suspected she could lift them from the floor and not move an inch from his embrace.

Finally they were kissing again. She had wanted this ever since they first exchanged conspiratorial whispers behind the decorative potted plants in the Marrywell assembly room.

At the time, he'd looked like adventure. She wasn't wrong—this was the best adventure she'd ever been on. But he was more than a passing moment. He was a person she admired, a gentleman whose compassionate heart always put others first, no matter how much he tried to hide it. He was a man full of depth and passion.

And he was kissing Matilda at last.

Of course she was ruined for all other men. Had been so, ever since the potted plants, long before she knew he was an earl and her temporary guardian. The only reason she cared about the opinions of his peers was because she wanted to make *friends*, not flirtations. When it came to future husbands, there was only one she wanted. The man whose mouth devoured hers, whose strong arms held her as though he feared she might dissipate like steam at any moment.

Marriage to him would be—

Gilbourne tore his lips from hers and all but dropped her onto the library floor.

"I'm sorry," he panted, swiping the back of his hand across his mouth as he backed away. "We can't. *I* can't. It shan't happen again."

Before she could catch her breath and her balance —much less formulate a response—he yanked open the door, darted into the corridor, and slammed the door behind him.

Matilda brought her own hand to her lips. Not to wipe the kiss away, but to press it into her soul. She would keep that moment and their kiss with her for always. And Gilbourne as well, if he'd let her.

Not that it was looking likely.

The backs of her eyes stung. She dropped her hand from her tender mouth to fumble for a tiny square of candied peel. Orange this time. One of her favorites. But even its sugared citrus flavor could not return the usual smile to her lips.

She wanted Gilbourne to apologize for casting her aside, not for kissing her senseless. He'd left her standing here in an empty room feeling small and rejected. Her shoulders slumped. The truth was, it didn't matter that he was more than good enough for Matilda.

She wasn't good enough for *him*.

Only when her face lost its splotchy flush and her tight throat returned to normal did she open the door and venture out into the corridor herself.

There was no sign of Gilbourne, of course. Who knew when or if she would see him next. He certainly wouldn't be sending away any more chaperones.

Nonetheless, she crept down the hall on silent feet. If he *was* lurking around one of these corners, she did not wish to startle him or send him scrambling away from her anew. She doubted she could weather that humiliation again.

There was no sign of Gilbourne. On her way back to her guest chamber, Matilda did stumble across the earl's silver-haired valet, Augustin, deep in conversation with the housekeeper, Mrs. Harris.

"*You* do it," Augustin was saying as he attempted to thrust an armful of tattered rags at Mrs. Harris. "I cannot."

"I categorically refuse." The housekeeper backed away as though the valet's well-tailored arms held hissing vipers rather than scraps of yellowed linen.

"You can't refuse," Augustin said desperately. "Everyone else has already refused, and you're the only one left."

"If you think for one moment that I could bear to put—" Mrs. Harris caught sight of Matilda and clamped her teeth together with an audible click.

Matilda stepped closer. "Is something wrong?"

"I'm away from my post, is what's wrong," said the housekeeper. Keeping her gaze averted from the beseeching valet, Mrs. Harris spun and stalked off without another word.

Augustin slumped his spine against the wall, cradling the old rags as though hugging a swaddled infant.

"What have you got there?" Matilda asked.

"Nothing." The valet closed his eyes and sighed. "Just some rubbish the earl wants me to burn."

Matilda stepped forward and peered closer at the scraps in Augustin's arms. The material appeared to have once been a white linen tablecloth or similar, until it had been torn into four surprisingly even strips. In any case, the scraps were far too serviceable to be destroyed in a fire.

"I'll take them," she offered.

Augustin's eyes flew open in obvious horror. "What?"

"I'm from the countryside," she explained. "We would never burn anything that could still be put to good use. If Mrs. Harris has no need for more rags, I could—"

"They're not rags," Augustin interrupted, his voice strangled.

Matilda frowned and reconsidered the pieces. The material was too thick and soft to be a table-cloth, nor was there quite enough fabric for that purpose.

She said slowly, "It's... a baby blanket?"

Terror flashed across the valet's face, followed immediately by a suspiciously blank expression.

"It *is* a baby blanket." Matilda stared at it in confusion. "Is there a baby?"

Augustin paused, then shook his head.

"*Was* there a baby? Is Gilbourne a father?"

The valet's face cleared, as though this were safer ground. "My lord has never had a wife or any children. He has no wish for either."

That made sense. In fact, the blanket was old enough for the white fabric to have yellowed. "Was this Gilbourne's blanket from when he was a baby?"

Augustin hesitated again. "No."

"Then who did it belong to?"

At her question, the valet's face once more resumed its hard-as-stone mask. He made no answer

ERICA RIDLEY

at all. Not even to tell her to mind her own business.

"How long have you been working for Gilbourne?" she asked.

"Since before my lord was born," Augustin answered with obvious pride. "I was valet to the earl's father."

"But... I thought he perished in an accident when the earl was small."

"When he was barely an adolescent, yes. When the lad was orphaned, my lord was sent to his godparents. Lady Stapleton was compassionate enough to insist no servant be summarily dismissed until such time as the new earl came of age and could make decisions for himself."

Matilda smiled. "I'm surprised Gilbourne waited until he was twenty-one to make decisions."

Augustin returned her smile. "My lord did not wait. As soon as his year of mourning ended, he appointed me as his personal valet. He was only thirteen. Ten more years would pass before he could take his seat in the House of Lords. But even at that age, his first decree was that any servant employed in any household in the earldom could remain under its protection for as long as he or she desired."

"That's sweet," she murmured. "He's a good man."

Augustin straightened his shoulders. "We are all more loyal than you can possibly imagine."

"Maybe I can," she said softly, then held out her palms. "Let me have the blanket."

"It's not a blanket anymore. These are rags now."

"Let me have the rags."

"They cannot be used for—"

"I won't. Whatever the history is, I'll be respectful."

The valet chewed his lips. "I was ordered to burn them."

"And you don't want to."

He winced. "None of us wants to."

"What if... *I* offer to burn them, and then 'accidentally' forget to do so?"

Augustin looked intrigued. "And when you leave?"

"I will likewise accidentally forget that these scraps were folded and stowed at the bottom of my wardrobe, where they will remain hidden in peace for as long as you wish it."

A look of abject relief crossed the valet's weathered face. He started to hand her what was left of the blanket, then paused. "Promise me, out loud, that you will burn these rags to ashes, as my lord has so ordered."

"Absolutely. I'll take them to my room right this second and throw them into the fire. They'll definitely not end up safe and sound in my wardrobe." She gave a melodramatic wink.

He winked back and handed her the scraps. "Splendid. You have done us all an enormous favor."

She hurried the rags upstairs to her guest chamber before Gilbourne could emerge from wherever he'd hidden himself and catch her in the act.

Once she was safely in her room with the door shut behind her, Matilda lay the limp pieces atop her bed and arranged them back into a whole. The edges weren't simply torn, she realized. They were *freshly* torn. And cleanly so. As if even the tearer had not wished to inflict undue harm.

She folded the pieces up and placed them in the back of her wardrobe as promised—or as *not* promised, as the case might be.

Curiosity burned inside of her. Whatever the story was, the servants clearly refused to gossip about it. Matilda just as clearly could not ask Gilbourne for clarification. She would have to resign herself to a permanent state of suspense.

Before closing the wardrobe door, she paused to take one last look at the unassuming folded scraps in the back corner.

A baby blanket.

A baby.

She longed for a family of her own one day, and could not imagine the grief she would experience if she lost a child. Losing her parents had been difficult enough. Going through that pain again...

Matilda shut the wardrobe door, blocking the blanket from view. She still felt its presence in the room. She needed to distract herself.

After glancing about, her eyes settled on the journal atop her bedside table. There, she could write in her diary. Not about the torn blanket—its secrets did not belong to her. But if she could dislodge some of the pain and confusion after Gilbourne's kiss and subsequent dismissal, perhaps she could regain a modicum of peace.

She scooped up the journal and a pencil and exited her guest chamber in search of a sunny parlor. Years ago, she used to cheer herself up by chatting with her parents, but now she had no family to turn to. A beautiful view and the warm light of the morning sun would have to be antidote enough.

Before she could begin her search for a suitable parlor, Matilda nearly collided with Mrs. Harris on the landing of the stairs.

The housekeeper gave her a sharp look. "I shan't speak further about whatever you think you overheard."

Matilda shook her head. "I won't ask you to."

"Good." Mrs. Harris reached for the ring of keys on her hip.

"Do you need help?" Matilda asked impulsively.

The housekeeper's eyebrows shot up. "I've been running this household for decades."

"I can't imagine managing a household even half this size," Matilda admitted.

"You'd learn," said Mrs. Harris.

"Would I, though? To Gilbourne's standards?" Matilda said doubtfully.

Mrs. Harris's expression turned considering. "Come on, then. If you're that bored, I'll show you the rounds. Any house can use an extra pair of hands."

Matilda grinned and held up her journal. "I'll take notes."

CHAPTER 23

*M*atilda spent the rest of the morning and all afternoon trailing Mrs. Harris up and down stairs and through almost every room of the house, save the earl's bedchamber—Matilda would only enter there if personally invited—and the earl's private study, where he was currently holed up and had been so all day.

She hadn't had time to dwell on his humiliating rejection of her after the best kiss of Matilda's life. She was too busy jotting notes in her journal of all the things Mrs. Harris told Matilda she'd need to be cognizant of in this or any similar household, were she to make a good match.

If Matilda had memorized a dizzying number of names at the card party the night before, that was only the beginning. She quickly learnt that over half of the servants hadn't even been present. There were more maids and footmen under this roof than a country miss could shake a stick at.

And a hierarchy for everyone! The housekeeper was the most important woman—next to the lady of the house, of course—and the butler the most important man, next to the earl. Buttons, despite being one of the newest members of staff, ranked as one of the highest. Apparently upstairs maids had higher standing than downstairs maids, and a *lady's* maid the most elevated of all.

Matilda asked a litany of increasingly impertinent questions. What were the tasks, the schedules, the wages, the unwritten rules? She wrote them all in her journal, separated by floor and section and punctuated with little charts to illustrate timetables and rules governing behavior, dress, and holidays.

That Mrs. Harris kept all of this information in her head was a stunning feat. The housekeeper could tell the keys apart on sight, knew at a glance if corners had been cut and whose head should roll. She could also scent when someone had gone above and beyond their duty, and deserved special recognition for their dedication and efficiency.

And this was just any old ordinary Wednesday! If this were the sort of house that hosted dinner parties and grand balls, or if the Earl of Gilbourne were the sort of man to up and rotate residences on a whim, there would be a thousand other considerations one would need to execute with flawless precision.

Matilda had never felt more imperfect in her life than as she scrawled line after barely legible line, trying her best to keep up with Mrs. Harris's detailed explanations.

They paused only for luncheon. As was apparently his custom, Gilbourne took his meal alone in his study, allowing only a trusted silent footman to slip inside its walls to deliver a heavy tray of covered silver dishes.

Matilda took her luncheon in the small dining room where the upstairs servants gathered, setting her journal aside to feast on savory pies and wincing at the purple indentation her pencil had made on her index finger from all her scribbling.

"Highly irregular," Mrs. Harris said of Matilda's presence at the servants' table, but the others were delighted to have her—especially once they discovered Matilda was trying to learn everything she could about the running of a household.

They talked over each other, forks in hand and food in mouths, giving enthusiastic explanations of each of their posts, how long they'd had it, and how it compared to previous situations before becoming employed by the Earl of Gilbourne.

Every one of them said they had never earned higher wages or been treated more fairly than here in this household, serving the earl.

"To be fair," said one of the chamber maids, "he'll threaten to sack you if you fail to meet expectations—"

"And it's not an idle threat," put in a footman. "There's been dozens who haven't lasted more than a month—"

"A week—"

"A day—"

Was that what had happened in the library? Matilda had failed to meet expectations, and had therefore been summarily sacked?

"But for those who fulfill their duty with efficiency and honor," Mrs. Harris continued, "my lord rewards such achievements with a home for a lifetime, and wages double or triple what you'd earn, even if you worked for the Prince Regent himself."

Augustin nodded. "No one is more loyal than the Earl of Gilbourne. When my mother was ill, he gave me two months' holiday, paid, to look after her."

"He gives an extra month's wages, every Christmas, so that we can purchase gifts for our loved ones."

"Or ourselves," added a maid with a cheeky grin.

"And he even lets us borrow books from his library, as long we return them in pristine condition."

"Oh, Lord, remember the time when Rhoda—"

"The uncut copy of *Castle Rackrent*! My lord was appalled!"

"I thought for certain she'd be sacked on the spot."

"So did she! Had her bag packed and ready before my lord was even home from Parliament and saw what she'd done."

"It was an accident. She's got clumsy fingers, is all."

"He wished to dismiss her for it?" Matilda asked.

They all stared at her as though she'd sprouted antennae.

"I just said it was an accident," said the footman. "My lord understands such things better than anyone. He says as long as no one is harmed, any accident can be forgiven."

"Docked her wages for the book, though," put in a maid. "And bought a fresh copy for the library."

"Rhoda never did go back in there," Augustin said with a chuckle.

It was this story that played in Matilda's head again and again all afternoon as she followed Mrs. Harris through the rest of her duties.

Anything could be forgiven, so long as no one was harmed.

Was that what she needed? To be forgiven? She *had* been the one to goad Gilbourne into that kiss. He'd told her it was supposed to be make-believe, and specifically instructed her to slap him before their lips made contact.

She'd climbed up him like a monkey instead,

latching onto his neck and demanding the very thing he hadn't intended to give.

That he hadn't stopped *her*... well. Perhaps he'd longed for that kiss just as fervently as Matilda had. Or perhaps he was too much of a gentleman to halt her in her tracks.

After all, she was his ward. He was saddled with her, like it or not. For three more weeks, anyway. Slightly less than. The days were disappearing like petals plucked from a flower. When the last one fluttered away... Matilda would be gone.

And so would her chance to prove herself worthy of a future with Gilbourne.

CHAPTER 24

$\mathcal{M}$atilda was just sitting down to supper —in the earl's primary dining room, at Mrs. Harris's fond insistence—when the earl himself strode through the door and took his seat at the head of the table.

Lord Gilbourne waited for Matilda to finish serving herself before he arranged his own plate.

Soon, she could stand the tension no longer. "I wanted to say I'm very—"

"We needn't discuss it," he interrupted, without glancing up from his plate of fish.

Well. All right, then.

She stared at him.

He stared at his plate, at his fork, at his goblet of wine. Anywhere but at Matilda.

She pressed her lips together and forced her gaze back to her own meal. Either Gilbourne didn't wish to allude to the matter whilst a footman stood in the shadows... or the earl did not believe the incident deserved any thought at all.

The rest of the meal passed in strained silence. Matilda made several attempts to engage Gilbourne in conversation. The weather, the newspaper, the books in his library.

Each parry was met with a grunt, and no flicker of interest or acknowledgement from his eyes whatsoever.

By the time the final course arrived, she had given up. Her plate of height-of-season fruit looked sweet and delicious, but she listlessly moved the pieces about with her fork.

"I suppose you're vexed we're not at some supper party."

Matilda whipped her head toward the earl. It had been so long since he'd spoken anything more eloquent than a sullen grunt that she'd almost forgot he was capable of the feat.

"I told you," she said quietly. "I would never ask you to do something you clearly despise."

Like attend a soirée.

Or kiss Matilda. Again.

"That will be disappointing news to at least two dozen hostesses," he said as if bored.

"W-what?" she stammered.

"You've received a prodigious number of invitations."

"*I* have?"

"At least five-and-twenty, by my last count."

"Liar," she breathed.

What on earth was his game? No one who was anyone had even heard of her. And even if they had, judging by her reception in Marrywell, an invitation to a private party would not be forthcoming.

"Liar?" He raised his dark brows and met her eyes at last. "If you cannot trust my word, do you want to see for yourself?"

She dropped her fork onto her plate and hurried to her feet. "Right this moment."

He laid his napkin beside his plate with care before rising to his own feet. "Then follow me."

Matilda followed so close behind she nearly rode on the back of his heels.

Inside Gilbourne's study, he strode toward a grand mahogany desk. Several stacks of correspondence sat on top. He lifted the largest of the towers and handed it to Matilda without further comment.

All of the wax seals were broken. And inside each folded missive was a rectangular invitation. Some were embossed, some were gilded, and some were plain. And every one of them was addressed to:

Lord Gilbourne
& Miss Dodd

SHE GASPED and pressed the pile to her chest, her vision suddenly blurry.

"Are you unhappy?" he asked with concern.

"Unhappy? I could just..." She returned the stack to his desk with care, then threw her arms around him and squeezed with all her might. "Thank you."

At first, he didn't move. Then one arm curved around her, and then the other. His embrace was loose—no one would confuse it with a proper hug—but she once again found herself back in his arms.

She pressed her cheek against his chest and held on tight. Was *this* what he had been doing, whilst she had spent a miserable day dying inside, believing he was ignoring and repulsed by her?

Had he been off in his study being *kind*, for God's sake?

"Surely *now* you can call me Matilda," she murmured into his cravat.

"I shall not."

She tilted her face up, resting her chin on his lapel so she could gaze up at him. "Miss Candied Orange?"

"No."

"Miss Sour Lemon?"

"No."

"Miss Citrus Peel?"

"No."

"Miss Eats-the-Part-Everyone-Else-Throws-Away?"

Unbelievably, the edges of his lips quirked.

It was not a proper smile, not fully, not really, but Matilda felt as though she'd battled a dragon and stolen its treasure all the same.

"How about 'Miss—'" she began.

"*Dodd*," he interrupted firmly. "I shall refer to you, now and always, as Miss Dodd."

She slid her arms about his neck and rose up on her toes. "You might at least have denied that my kiss tasted of sour lemon."

His gaze dropped to her lips. "You know very well that you taste only of sweet—" He stiffened, removed her arms from his person, and pushed her away. "That's enough, Miss Dodd."

She frowned. "But you—"

"—are complying with my duty as your guardian. Nothing more. The more potential suitors you meet, the sooner you'll be out of my hair. This isn't a favor to you. It's expediency for me."

Oh. *Ouch.*

He didn't want another kiss. He wanted her to marry someone else, and disappear from his life as swiftly as possible.

She slumped into the armchair before his desk, pulling the stack of invitations back into her lap. This time, the missives felt dull and heavy.

"Thank you all the same," she murmured. "I appreciate your efforts when faced with such an annoyance."

"Not nearly off-putting enough," he muttered, as he sank gracefully into his own chair. "I don't dislike you, Miss Dodd. But there is no room for you in my life."

"Are you never lonely?" she asked, then wished she hadn't. It wasn't the right question.

She didn't want him to keep her close out of loneliness or apathy. She wanted him to *choose* her. She wanted to be with someone who could have anyone in the entire world and who nonetheless wanted *her* above all others. As viscerally as she yearned for him.

"I lost my right to complain about loneliness long ago," he said lightly.

She frowned. "How can anyone lose the right to hate loneliness?"

He smiled, but it was not the smile she had longed to see. It was a cold smile, a hard smile, a brittle smile. A smile that was secretly a frown. Or a sob. A smile of masked sadness, deeper than she could imagine.

"If I tell you, will you leave it be?" he asked.

She set down the invitations and nodded, folding her hands in her lap.

He pointed at his cheek. "Do you know how I got my scars?"

She tilted her head. "An accident, presumably."

He laughed. It was worse than the smile. Harsh and discordant and self-deprecating. "An accident? It was many things, but not, perhaps, *that.*"

She forced herself not to reach for his hand. "I know what it is like to lose one's parents. The worst pain imaginable. A year of mourning barely takes the edge off. One feels as though—"

"You haven't the least notion how I feel," he snapped. "I lost my parents, yes. And my little brother. I was twelve. Oliver was eight. Too old, I told him, to be dragging about a silly baby blanket, like an infant fresh from the cradle."

Matilda's heart clenched. The blanket at the bottom of her wardrobe. It must have belonged to Oliver.

"Father thought it foolish as well, and there was nothing I would not do to impress him. So I needled Oliver every chance I got. He had the blanket with him that day because we were going on holiday to visit my godparents. Oliver was deathly afraid of water. Every time we neared a bridge, his eyes would fill up with tears and he would hide himself under that blanket to block out the sight until the danger was gone."

Matilda's heart went out to poor Oliver. He'd feared the water as much as she feared spiderwebs and rejection. Matilda's diced peels were her blanket. Sometimes, one took comfort wherever one could find it.

"I'd had enough." Gilbourne's lip curled in self-flagellation. "The next bridge we neared, I snatched the blanket from Oliver's white-knuckled hands. Laughing, I dangled it outside the open-top barouche, and threatened to toss it into the raging river below."

Oh no. Matilda held her breath, her skin crawling with trepidation.

"Father was driving. He loved to drive. But at that moment, on that bridge, because of my behavior, he turned and glanced over his shoulder to see what I was doing." Gilbourne swallowed visibly. "That's all it took."

"What happened?" she whispered in horror.

"A stray cat, of all things, darted before the horses, who reared in alarm. They bumped into each other and lost their footing. The outermost horse put a shoulder through the railing. If the wood had held... But the bridge was old, its railing rotted. The sickening sound of the wood splintering was nothing compared to what happened next."

Matilda's stomach turned.

"The horses went over the edge first, followed by the rest of the carriage. Because there was no roof, we tumbled free, all four of us, landing face-first in the water and on the rocks. The carriage came crashing down on top of us, pulled by its yoke to the horses. I heard the gurgle of my brother's last breath, as he died in the very manner he most feared."

"Gilbourne..."

"They all died. Both of the horses and my entire family. Because of me. I broke eight bones that day, and had to be told later they thought they'd have to break my fingers as well in order to pry Oliver's blanket out of my hand. Even in death, I wouldn't let him have it."

"No," she burst out. "That's not what happened."

"I was there." His eyes were haunted. "I'll never forget a single scream."

"Those may be the facts, but it wasn't your *fault*. It was an accident, Gilbourne. A terrible, horrible accident. You cannot possibly blame—"

A knock sounded at the open study door, startling them both. "Milord?"

"Come in," Gilbourne said as if he hadn't been in the midst of reliving the most traumatic moment of his life.

Or, perhaps more accurately, as if he never *ceased* reliving his worst moments, and must muddle through his responsibilities and his duty despite the tears and the screams and the crunch and the pain echoing constantly in his head.

"It's a parcel for Miss Dodd," the footman explained apologetically. "Sent from Madame Theroux."

"The first gown," Gilbourne said briskly. "How fitting. Choose an invitation to accept, then have Buttons prepare you for an outing. I'll meet you at the front door in two hours."

She stared at him. "B-but—"

"Make haste," he said sharply. "With luck, your future suitor awaits."

CHAPTER 25

a fortnight of whirlwind invitations later, Matilda was just about to ring for a bath to be brought to her bedchamber when a knock sounded on the door.

When she answered the call, a footman handed her a parcel. "From Madame Theroux."

"Thank you, Isaiah."

Matilda closed the door and carried the parcel over to her bed. It was supposed to be the final gown of the new wardrobe Gilbourne had commissioned for her, but the parcel seemed unusually large, even for an evening gown.

She unknotted the twine and opened the paper to reveal not only the most beautiful gown she'd ever seen... but also a large quantity of lacy, frilly nothings, with matching stockings and garters. *Undergarments*.

"I shan't be needing those any time soon," she murmured wryly, and stuffed them in the back of her wardrobe without investigating further.

The first few days after Gilbourne had kissed her and then utterly rejected her, he had acted as though

neither event had occurred. He was so overly solici-
tous and polite, it had made her want to scream.

Fortunately, he could not keep up such behavior
for long. They soon settled into a pattern that closely
resembled good friends. It was not what Matilda
wanted, but better than she'd feared. They took every
meal together, and when Gilbourne was not at Parliament or in his study, he was either spiriting
Matilda to yet another soirée, or tucked away with
her in his library, reading side-by-side in compan-
ionable silence. She did not pester him about what he
had revealed of his past, respecting her promise to let
it lie.

Buttons rushed into the bedchamber. "Was that
the final gown from Madame Theroux?"

"Indeed." Matilda held up the pink crepe frock,
draped over a dark rose slip.

Flowery vandykes of black velvet ornamented the
bottom hem, above three folds of extravagant lace in
large rouleaux. There was a matching headdress, a
matching rose scarf with black silk fringe, matching
armlets, and black chamois leather gloves and
dancing slippers, each ornamented with rosettes of
white chenille.

Buttons squealed and clapped her hands,
bouncing on her heels. "Have you ever seen a gown
so fine? You will be the most elegant of them all!"

Matilda hoped Gilbourne would feel the same.
And that perhaps tonight, he would cease thrusting
her into the paths of eligible bachelors and decide to
claim her for himself.

Or at least *consider* the possibility.

"I ordered the bath," Buttons said. "And I know
just what to do with your hair. I'll go and put the
curling tongs above the fire."

With butterflies gathering in Matilda's stomach,

she allowed herself to be bathed and dressed and primped. One might have supposed she'd be used to being made over by now, but every evening, it was as though the fairy godmother had arrived anew to turn the piglet into a princess.

She could scarcely believe that she'd attended two full weeks of balls and soirées and dinner parties. Or that only one week remained before her twenty-first birthday, when it would all come crashing down.

"Stop it," she muttered to herself. Until Gilbourne, she'd been so looking forward to her twenty-first birthday, and the freedom and adventure her inheritance would provide.

Just because her guardian's birthday gift would be a boot to the backside and the sound of his front door slamming behind her did not lessen her future adventures in any way.

Except... it felt like it *did*. Matilda no longer wanted to travel the world as an independent spinster—if indeed her inheritance would cover that to begin with. What had once seemed an unimaginably large number, she now realized to be a modest sum that ought to be budgeted wisely and spent sparingly.

Nonetheless, she'd relinquish every shilling in a heartbeat if she could exchange that old dream for her new one.

She wanted Gilbourne. Even if there was no large household in London. Even if they were penniless. Even if the only way to be together would be to remove to her parents' minuscule cottage in the small hamlet of Rutland, where their closest neighbors really would be piglets. At least she and Gilbourne would have each other.

But he didn't want her. Not here or anywhere. In or out of this gorgeous, fashionable gown.

She fumbled for her reticule. Of her previously

abundant hoard, only a trio of tiny candied peels remained. She popped all three into her mouth at once.

"I'm ready," she told Buttons.

Her maid threaded a quartet of flowers into Matilda's elaborately braided hair arrangement and added the decorative headdress.

"*Now* you're ready," she pronounced, beaming with satisfaction and pride.

"Thank you, Buttons."

Matilda hurried down the stairs to the parlor where Lord Gilbourne would be awaiting her. She had never arrived first, no matter how quickly she tried to rush her preparations. He was always standing there, stoic, hands behind his back, every inch of him tailored to absolute perfection, a fashion plate come to life.

And when his eyes caught sight of Matilda, his gaze sharpened and shone with heat.

It was this that gave her hope. The knowledge that his first glance at her every night took his breath away the way every glimpse of him did to her.

They arrived at tonight's ball like every other: with Matilda's gloved fingers curved about Gilbourne's elbow, their invitation in his free hand. Normally, Matilda's reticule of candied orange and lemon peels hung from her other wrist, but tonight she'd left it at home. No sense carrying about an empty pouch for no reason.

Their names were announced in short order. She and Gilbourne swept into an enormous ballroom filled with chandeliers and music and people.

As always, she could feel the muscles of his arm tense beneath her fingers, through three layers of fabric. No one else would know by looking at him how he despised being the center of attention, even for a moment.

Or rather, he *always* looked as though he'd rather be doing literally anything besides participating in a society event. Which made his mask look more like unapologetic misanthropy than the shy discomfort of a man who felt defined by the raised scars criss-crossing half his face.

He thought his face marked him as a killer and an outcast, but when Matilda looked at him, all she saw was a compassionate soul who had suffered more than enough and deserved to let himself find happiness.

For the moment, however, everyone else in the ballroom had just discovered *them*.

Peers surrounded Gilbourne as if they hadn't just seen him earlier that day or the day before, so eager were they to compliment him on his forceful speeches in the House of Lords and the positive so-cial changes his hard-won bills set in motion throughout England.

The unmarried lords also took the opportunity to sign Matilda's dance card before the bevy of waiting bucks and dandies could beat them to it.

Ever since she'd first arrived at a ball with Gilbourne at her side and one of Madame Theroux's creations enveloping her frame, Matilda had been in high demand. A dream come true—for someone else.

As much as she enjoyed all the dancing, she wished Gilbourne were one of her partners. He had the advantage of traveling with her in the same car-riage every night, during which he could lay claim to any minuet or waltz he pleased.

He never did.

So tonight, just like every other night, her dance card filled with name after name until there were no free sets left. And not one of those names belonged to the tense, stone-faced earl at her side.

"Five minutes," he said. "A new record."

"Have you been timing my invitations to dance?" she said in surprise.

"They're too eager. It's unbecoming. Jackals, all."

"You introduced me to each one of them."

"I believed they possessed a modicum of decorum."

"You believed they were terrified of you, and you were right. It took a full week for them to stop trembling every time they ventured close enough to ask me for a dance."

"I never stopped them," he protested.

"You glare a hole right through their faces."

He was unrepentant. "If they cannot tolerate casual visual contact, how can they expect to make you a proper husband?"

"They're inviting me to the dance floor, not to the altar."

"That's the first step," he muttered. "It's in the rulebook."

"And besides, there's nothing casual about making visual contact with you. Your glare reaches through their eye sockets and rattles their skulls."

He sent her a sharp look. "Is that how it feels when I look at you?"

"No," she said softly. "Your gaze feels like a caress. Sometimes warm, sometimes soft, and sometimes highly improper."

His eyes glittered wickedly before he blinked his obvious interest away and sent her a look of icy disdain. "Such flights of fancy."

"Is it? Here comes Lord Thackery to collect me for the first dance. Try not to bore a hole through the back of his head with your glaring."

Lord Thackery sent a wary look toward the earl. "Gilbourne, fine day. And you, Miss Dodd. Exquisite as always." He lifted Matilda's gloved fingers to his lips, then placed them on his arm. "Shall we?"

"Please. You are all that is kind."

Gilbourne was not gazing at Lord Thackery as though the marquess was kind. Gilbourne glowered at him as though he longed to peel him like an orange and squeeze the pulp between his fingers.

Lord Thackery increased his pace. "Come, dear heart. Shall we find our spot?"

He did not say *far away from your guardian* aloud, but the marquess's champagne-shined boots all but scurried across the parquet in his eagerness to put space between them and the Earl of Gilbourne.

CHAPTER 26

$\mathcal{T}$hree hours later, scant moments before the final dance set of the night, their hostess announced a ten-minute interlude for the musicians and anyone else who needed a brief respite.

Matilda was grateful for a moment to herself. Well, not to *herself*, exactly—she was still on her feet in a crowded ballroom. But at least she needn't parry flirtatious overtures from suitors she was uninterested in, striking that careful balance between friendly and not *too* friendly. It was frankly exhausting.

They were down to the final two songs. The evening was to end with waltzing. Lord Thackery had claimed a second set. When he'd signed his name on her card for the second time, Lord Thackery had seemed coy. She hoped he didn't plan on proposing.

Matilda made her way to the refreshment table for a glass of ratafia. The moment she neared, the queue seemed to swirl around her like circling sharks. She could not help but tense.

"I scarcely recognize you," said a young lady who had been at the matchmaking festival. "You look ravishing. Quite the transformation from Marrywell, if I might be so blunt."

Matilda relaxed. "Thank you. I owe any and all radiance to the skillful hands of Madame Theroux... and the largesse of my guardian, Lord Gilbourne."

"Madame Theroux?" said a second girl. "I've been contemplating adding my name to her waiting list."

"You won't regret it," Matilda promised. "As you can see with your own eyes, she performs miracles with thread and cloth."

The other young ladies peppered her with questions about this fashion or that. Occasionally, gentlemen slipped their way into the throng and attempted to secure a preemptive spot on Matilda's dance card for the next soirée.

One of the young women—Lady Tabitha Kerr, the only soul to have been kind to Matilda in Marrywell —batted the last of the young bucks away.

She grinned at Matilda. "By the looks of things, I'd wager you'd have half a dozen marriage proposals in hand tonight alone, if the Earl of Gilbourne's glare wasn't actively turning your suitors into piles of ash."

Matilda's cheeks heated. "He's... protective, that's all."

"Is that what you call it?" Lady Tabitha said mildly, and made a production of fanning her bodice. "If these ladies were after your earl, you'd have more knives in your back than pin cushions have needles."

"I don't know why they *wouldn't* be after him," Matilda said with heat. "He's the most eligible bachelor in this ballroom."

Lady Tabitha lowered her fan, her eyes sparkling. "Is that right?"

"But he's not for you," Matilda said quickly. "You're already betrothed."

Lady Tabitha grimaced. "Please do not remind me."

Matilda's heart twisted. The only thing worse than the man one loved not returning the emotion, would be the torture of a life sentence leg-shackled to a person one could not even abide.

"Why are you marrying him, if you'd rather not?" she asked.

"'Rather not' is an understatement," Lady Tabitha said beneath her breath, then lifted her fan to hide both her and Matilda's mouths from view. "Decades ago, Viscount Oldfield fought with my father in the war. Father said the viscount was like family, and betrothed me to him upon my birth in order to make the ties permanent."

"But... the viscount is old enough to *be* your father!"

Lady Tabitha snorted. "Do you think any debutante in here would hesitate to marry a duke or a prince because of a difference in age?"

"Can't you say no? Do you not yet have your majority?"

"I do. But no, my hands are tied. My father is unwell and it is quite literally his dying wish to see Oldfield and I properly wed whilst he's still alive to witness the ceremony. If the viscount had found a match elsewhere in time..."

"But if mercenary young women would marry a turnip for a title, how was Lord Oldfield possibly unlucky in love?"

"He wasn't looking for love," Lady Tabitha said dryly. "His betrothal to me gave him the freedom to sow his wild oats freely, since it was common knowledge he was already spoken for. Are you familiar with the name Reuben Medford?"

"The infamous rakehell?"

"A married man, now. Medford is Oldfield's nephew—and for many years, his ward. With an example like that to follow, it's no wonder the man turned out as he did. Oldfield turned fifty last year, and he's still leering at debutantes younger than I am."

"Does he not want to marry you?" Matilda asked in confusion.

"His marriage to me is irrelevant. Many titled men don't curb their outside interests just because they've taken a wife. Usually, they try to be discreet about their affairs, but the truth of the matter is… The less time Oldfield is home with me, the better for both of us."

Matilda repressed a shudder. "I'm so sorry."

"Don't be. I'm told it's an enviable match." Lady Tabitha's eyes were sad, but the line of her jaw resolute.

"What's this?" came a loud voice right behind them.

Lady Tabitha lowered her fan to her side as she and Matilda spun about to see who had interrupted them.

Miss Bernice Charlton. Of course.

"I see our little piglet wriggled out of her sty and into the hands of a modiste," Miss Charlton observed, to the appreciative tittering of her entourage.

"That's enough, Bernice," Lady Tabitha snapped. "Take your claws somewhere else."

"Oh no, girls," Miss Charlton cooed, pressing her hand to her bosom. "I've been dismissed by the one person in this ballroom whose marriage prospects are so dismal, her ill luck rivals that of our little piglet."

Matilda's fingers curled into fists. "I'd rather be a piglet than a shrew."

Lady Tabitha stepped forward. "I mean it, Bernice. I won't hear another cross word against—"

"Looking forward to your marriage night, are you, Lady Tabitha? Just think of all the heirs and spares you'll soon beget. There goes your beloved now. I'll wave for him to come and collect you."

"No! Don't—"

But it was too late. Miss Charlton batted her eyes at Viscount Oldfield, which brought him running. He was visibly annoyed to be pawned off onto his betrothed instead.

"I suppose the waltz will begin at any moment." He gave a last, lascivious glance at Miss Charlton's bodice. "Come, Tabitha. We might as well take our places."

He swept Lady Tabitha away.

"Oh dear," said Miss Charlton with her most saccharine voice. "The shamelessly depraved roué who would tup any creature that moved didn't even *glance* at our little piglet. I suppose even a well-made gown cannot cover up the stench of a country cow pile."

"Your flimsy insults cannot wound me," Matilda said through clenched teeth. "You're patently wrong. My dance cards have been full for a fortnight—"

"Because all the lords wish to curry favor with your earl," Miss Charlton interrupted, flashing her teeth in a vicious smile. "My mistake, he's not your earl at all, is he? I notice *his* name is never on your card. Ah, well. I'll be certain to congratulate him on his excellent taste and good judgment once I become his countess."

She flounced off before Matilda could formulate a retort.

Lord Gilbourne was at her side within seconds. "What's wrong? You're making a dreadful expression."

Matilda reached for the reticule at her wrist, then ground her teeth as she remembered she'd left it at home because it had finally run empty. "That's my orange-peel-cravings expression. I get peevish when I go too long without sugar."

Gilbourne pulled a small pouch from his pocket. "Would candied lemon and lime peels do?"

She grabbed the pouch from him and stuffed one of each into her mouth. "Have you been carrying this around all night?"

"All *fort*night," he admitted. "I wasn't certain when or if you'd run out, but I wanted to be ready."

"You've saved my life," she said with feeling. "*Again*."

He crossed his arms. "Now will you tell me what happened?"

"I told you," she muttered. "One mustn't speak ill of others."

"And I'm telling *you*," he replied. "If you don't speak ill with full detail here and now, I will smite every person in this ballroom until I find the one who has hurt you."

"It's nothing," Matilda said quickly. "Miss Charlton sees me as a country bumpkin playing dress-up as if I were a fine lady."

"You *are* a fine young lady."

"But mostly a country bumpkin," Matilda said with a sigh. "My new wardrobe is a thin disguise. She said the only reason anyone takes pity and dances with me is to impress *you*. Not me."

Gilbourne's eyes darkened. "If you think any name on your dance card wouldn't duel me at dawn for a chance to—"

"There you are!" Lord Thackery burst between them, panting. "I looked everywhere for you, Miss Dodd. This is our second set. It's to be a waltz."

"No." Gilbourne brushed Lord Thackery away with the back of his arm, then forcefully linked arms with Matilda. "I'm certain you've misremembered. This is *my* set with my ward."

Matilda and Lord Thackery both stared at him.

"But—I signed my name on her card right in front of you! If you'll take a look, you'll see—"

"I see that if you don't get out of our way," Gilbourne growled, "your knees will soon no longer be intact."

Lord Thackery swallowed visibly and backed away, palms up. "Your waltz. Miss Dodd, I'll take the first one tomorrow night. If your guardian so allows it."

Gilbourne didn't bother responding to him. He led Matilda to the crowded dance floor instead. A sea of whispers followed in their wake.

Before she could catch her breath, Bernice Charlton swooped in front of them, her face an angry mask.

"Do you think you're better than me?" she hissed at Matilda.

"The dirt at the bottom of Miss Dodd's boot is better than you," Gilbourne said coolly. He waved his hand as if shooing away a pesky gnat.

Miss Charlton blanched. "But... I..."

"I don't care about you, and neither does Miss Dodd. If you so much as *think* my ward's name in the future, you will live to deeply regret it. Please remove yourself from our path, and stay gone."

The crowd tittered at the unflinching rejection. Miss Charlton flushed with humiliation and fled the dance floor, her bewildered partner trailing close behind her.

"There," Gilbourne said with satisfaction. "I daresay she won't venture round again."

"That was glorious," Matilda said, breathless at witnessing such a brutal cut direct to the woman who had lorded her superiority over Matilda from the moment they first met. "Thank you."

His eyes glittered. "Where were we?"

The music started and Gilbourne swung her into the first steps. He was as masterful a dancer here as he had been that afternoon in the library, when they'd waltzed without music.

"Miss Charlton deserved her set-down, but you were unnecessarily rude to that sweet Lord Thackery," she informed him.

"Was I?" Gilbourne replied as if bored.

"You frightened him off."

"Hopefully for good." The earl's eyes flashed with satisfaction.

"I thought you refused to dance in public," Matilda insisted.

"I refuse to dance at all," Gilbourne replied.

"What are we doing right now, then?"

"I'm asking myself that very question." His eyes were hot on hers. "None of my rules seem to matter when it comes to you."

Her throat dried. "Because we keep breaking rule number one: 'no touching'?"

"And you've never paid any heed to rule number two: 'do as I say.'"

"I'm dancing with you, just as you commanded," she reminded him.

He arched a brow. "You say that as though I should have asked nicely."

"It's worth consideration."

He shrugged. "Your list was full."

"You've had plenty of opportunities to be the first name."

"This way is better," he assured her. "I get to waltz

ERICA RIDLEY

with you *and* I haven't broken my streak of never signing anyone's dance card."

She rolled her eyes. "You're incorrigible."

He grinned at her unrepentantly.

Gasps echoed around them. The unprecedented sight of the Earl of Gilbourne smiling dazzled everyone in the ballroom.

"Be careful," she warned him. "You're ruining your reputation."

"They know I hate them all," he said cheerfully. "One smile at you doesn't mean I'll show an ounce of pity at the next Parliamentary session. If anything, it'll sting worse, now that they know I *can* be reasonable… and choose not to."

"How many of them flee the House of Lords every night in tears?"

"On a good day?" He blinked at her innocently. "All of them."

She shook her head, but was unable to tear her gaze from his. Blast it all, she *loved* this relentless, brooding, powerful, impossible man. Her smile fell.

He didn't love *her*. If he felt any soft feelings toward her at all, they didn't matter. Rules came first. And the one rule he would stick to was the one where they waved goodbye the moment she came into her inheritance.

One week from today.

CHAPTER 27

$\mathcal{S}$ix days later, Titus was at home in his study drafting a speech for the House of Lords, when the cursed papers arrived.

Official confirmation from Titus's solicitor: all of the documents pertaining to Miss Dodd's inheritance were in order. At midnight tonight, she would become an independent heiress. The moment she turned twenty-one, she was no longer his.

Er, his *ward*. No longer his ward.

Or his.

Not that she ever truly had been. From the moment they'd arrived in London and he'd taken her to Madame Theroux's instead of straight home, he'd known he was opening Pandora's box.

His ward had become an overnight sensation. Which just went to prove what a box of cabbage feathers the members of the beau monde were. Miss Dodd had *always* been sensational. With or without fine French fashions.

He'd danced with her to make her smile—and, yes, because he wanted to, had been dying to, for a fortnight straight. Ever since that night, Titus had been paying the price for his rash behavior.

If Madame Theroux's gowns had turned Miss Dodd into a princess, her waltz with the infamously unengageable earl made her a goddess. Her status skyrocketed the moment they took that first step. At the new threat, suitors everywhere redoubled their efforts. Every single surface of Titus's house was filled with flowers for the indomitable Miss Dodd, from dozens of hopeful beaux.

Although Titus had begrudgingly informed his ward that she was free to entertain callers as she wished, to his knowledge she hadn't responded to a single poem or bouquet sent by one of her countless suitors.

Miss Dodd spent her time with Titus instead.

Early morning walks before the rest of the ton was awake. Afternoons in the library, their stocking feet up on each other's cushions. Candlelit dinners with wine and strawberries.

It felt like a courtship, though it was nothing of the sort. For one, Titus refused to court anyone. And for two, he was actually enjoying himself. Oh, not the endless ballrooms, where he was forced to watch her flit from the embrace of one dunder-beard to another. And not the long hours he was forced to spend away from her in Parliament, pleading cases before the House of Lords instead of being home with Miss Dodd, as he would have preferred.

But whenever the two of them occupied the same space... Whenever she so much as strolled down the corridor past an open doorway, through which he happened to be gazing... The sight of her filled him with—

He didn't *know* what. He didn't have words for this. Her face made him happy and dizzy and caused his stomach to flutter. The sound of her voice soothed his soul, and the sound of her laughter filled him with sunlight.

And tomorrow morning, that light would extinguish from his life forever.

How Titus wished he hadn't destroyed Oliver's blanket! With Miss Dodd gone, the house would feel unbearably empty. Instead of launching himself out of bed to stroll with her beneath the colors of dawn, he would curl into the tightest ball he could make and wish that he were someone else.

Someone who could've kept her.

Someone who deserved a wife and a family.

Someone worthy of love.

He shoved the inheritance papers aside and reached for his pen and ink. If tomorrow was to be their last day together, he would make it one to remember. A party. She wouldn't expect that. A celebration, of her birthday, of her independence, of...

Well, the truth was, Titus didn't much feel like celebrating any of it. But he would, for her. Because it was what she wanted. She deserved to make her own decisions, to steer her own ship.

To live a happy life, free from the peril of his love.

Quickly, he dashed off the invitations to anyone who had ever made her smile. Oh, very well, and anyone who had sent invitations or... flowers. Never let it be said that Titus attempted to stifle her in any form.

No door would open to Miss Charlton and her friends, of course. Titus had given her the cut direct at the first available opportunity. She had not dared to so much as glance in their direction since.

This would be a *happy* party. Happy, happy, happy. A fun, happy celebration.

That Titus would hate every second of.

Worth it, if it brought a smile to Miss Dodd's lips.

He sent the invitations off with a footman, then went in search of his ward. Not to tell her about the party —it would be a surprise, on the morrow. But to see her. To smell her scent whilst he still could.

He found her in the entryway, greeting... his housekeeper? Who had apparently just arrived from... somewhere? For some reason?

"Here you are," Miss Dodd was saying as she handed Mrs. Harris a familiar ring of keys. "There were no problems."

"I knew there wouldn't be," Mrs. Harris replied as she tied on an apron and slipped the keys into its front pocket.

"You knew *what* wouldn't be a problem?" Titus demanded.

Both women jumped guiltily.

He glowered at them. "Explain yourselves."

"Mrs. Harris had an emergency," Miss Dodd blurted out. "She was only gone for five days."

"Five days!"

"We didn't want to bother you—"

"You're so busy, my lord."

"So many more important things for you to worry about," his ward said in a rush.

"And Matilda knows the inner workings of this house almost as well as I do."

"Miss Dodd," he corrected automatically, then blinked. "She what?"

"I've been practicing," his ward explained with an embarrassed smile. "Mrs. Harris said that if I could run this house, I could run any man's house. I admit I took it as a bit of a challenge."

He wished she wasn't thinking about any man but him.

"How did you do it at all?" he asked in bafflement. "When did you sleep?"

"He truly didn't notice my absence," Mrs. Harris said in wonder. "I don't know if I should be offended for myself or thrilled for you, Matilda. I'll settle on both."

Miss Dodd hugged her. "I could not have done so without your guidance."

"No touching," Titus snapped.

"That's your rule, not Mrs. Harris's," Matilda said without removing her embrace from his housekeeper.

Who impertinently hugged his ward right back.

"If you do anything like that again, I'll give you the sack," Titus warned Mrs. Harris. "No such decisions should have been made without consulting the master of the house."

"Household decisions?" Mrs. Harris asked archly. "You explicitly entrusted the running of this house to me, which involves delegating as I see fit. I oversee both the upstairs and the downstairs maids—"

"My ward is not a maid!"

"—and as long as every task is completed according to your standards, you personally instructed me to use my judgment as required, and to refrain from bothering you unnecessarily. If you fear I've taken advantage monetarily, do not worry. I've already deducted the missing days from my wages."

"Oh, keep the wages," Titus grumbled. "And cease the pontificating. Go and do whatever it is that you should have been doing all along. I need to speak to my ward."

Mrs. Harris curtseyed and hurried off—but not before tossing a wink at Miss Dodd, who fluttered her eyelashes at Titus winningly.

How could he possibly maintain his pique when assaulted with a smile as beautiful as that?

"You wanted to see me?" his ward asked innocently.

He glared at her. "Your papers are in order."

Her forehead furrowed. "What papers?"

"Your inheritance papers. The funds will be in an account in your name when the banks open tomorrow morning. You'll wake up a fully independent woman."

Her smile faltered. "I see."

"We're almost out of each other's hair," he added.

"You were never in my hair," she said softly. "I've enjoyed my time with you."

So had he. But the words were lodged deep inside his heart, which was walled in with stones so heavy, even Titus could not find a way through.

"I suppose I should pack." She glanced toward the stairs. "Buttons will help me."

"You can take her."

"Thank you. I think she might like that. And I'll appreciate a friendly face."

Titus turned his away. No one had ever accused his visage of being appealing. Or friendly.

"I might as well leave after breakfast," she offered. "It's a long drive back home."

"Stay through teatime," he said quickly. The guests were supposed to arrive in the morning, but to the ton, "morning" could mean one or two o'clock in the afternoon.

"Teatime," she repeated. "All right. I suppose I could do that."

He didn't want her to leave at all. He wanted her to stay for breakfast and tea and supper, and keep staying until his birthday, and then stay to her next birthday, and every day after that. He wanted to take that key ring from Mrs. Harris, then lock himself and

Miss Dodd in his bedchamber and never come out again, Parliament be damned.

God help him, Titus couldn't bear to lose her. But nor could he stop her. She was free now.

"You must be knackered," he said. "It'll be a long day tomorrow. Come with me to the library. You can borrow any book you please, for as long as you wish. And if you'd like to start reading tonight... I have wine and two goblets."

She tilted her head, her eyes unusually unreadable. "I would like that."

But when he poured the wine, she didn't drink it. She lay in semi-repose atop a chaise, swirling and swirling the burgundy liquid in its crystal goblet, staring into its depths as though the answer to a mystery lay inside her glass.

"What's wrong?" he demanded.

She glanced up from her glass, the corners of her eyes furrowing with sadness. "I'm realizing how much I will miss you."

He felt each word like a punch to his solar plexus.

"I'll miss you as well," he admitted gruffly. "You needn't leave tomorrow, if you're not ready yet."

Her eyebrows shot heavenward. "I thought you were eager to have your life back to normal."

"I no longer know what 'normal' is." Scratch that. He knew exactly what he wanted: the *new* normal, not the old one. He wanted moments like these. Just him and her. And no shortage of torrid kisses. "Although you might not believe it, Matilda, I do find—"

She gasped and set down her wine. "What did you just call me?"

Oops.

"Tilda?" he guessed.

A smile rose to her lips. "I'll take it."

"Tilly? Tilly-bean? Miss Orange Peel? Mattie-Mat-Mat?"

She burst out laughing. "Did you write them all down?"

"I never forget a single word you say. I'll *never* forget anything about you."

She stared at him, eyes wide and questioning.

He set his wine aside and reached for her. She came to him eagerly. Their mouths collided. Their souls, their hearts. He tumbled onto the chaise with her, crushing her to him. Trying his best to hold her so tight, she would never leave him behind.

But he knew, come morning, if she asked him to...

He would stand back and wave goodbye.

CHAPTER 28

*M*atilda sank her fingers into the Earl of Gilbourne's soft dark hair. "And me? Am I still to call you Lord Gilbourne?"

"My name is Titus," he said between kisses. "But you may call me anything you wish."

She smiled against his lips. "Anything?"

"Maybe not Gilly-Gil-Gil or your darling Gilly-bear," he admitted. "At least not in public. Let's start with Titus and see where we go from there."

"Titus," she mouthed.

His lips slanted over hers, and conversation was forgotten.

She would never tire of the warmth of his body snuggled against hers, or the possessive safety of finding herself once again wrapped in his strong embrace. His tongue tasted of rich burgundy, and his hands felt divine as they caressed her face and her back.

The chaise longue was barely big enough to contain the two of them, but with their arms about each other and their legs intertwined, their bodies had molded into one. She was in heaven.

Soon, his kisses strayed from her lips and began

to trace a path down her throat to her collarbone, then just above the visible swell of her bosom.

"Is this a seduction?" she murmured into his hair.

He lifted his face, his dilated eyes smoldering. "I've never been more seduced."

Neither had Matilda, but that had never been in question. She gave up on subtext and phrased her thoughts more boldly. "No, I mean... Is this a proposal?"

The earl reared away from her as if her bodice had caught on fire, his expression nothing short of terrified. "I cannot offer you marriage. I'm sorry. You should go. I can't be what you want."

"You already *are* what I want." She grasped his lapels and pulled him back toward her. "I would rather take what you can give than not have you at all."

"Even if I cannot be your husband?"

"Even then."

His expression was tortured. "I should be strong enough to walk away."

She reached for him. "Please don't. For me. For both of us."

He let out a ragged breath, then his mouth captured hers once more. Each kiss intense almost to the point of desperation. As if he had feared for a moment that they'd already shared their final kiss. No, that wasn't it. The truth was, Titus knew without a doubt that this would be their only passionate encounter, and he didn't want to miss out on a single kiss. Matilda had been right all along: her time with Titus was to be her greatest adventure after all.

And all adventures must come to an end.

She kissed him while she still had him, trying to commit every detail to memory. The solid heat of his body, the sweet taste of his tongue, the softness of his hair, the slight tickle of half his stubbled jaw as his seductive kisses sank toward her bosom once more.

"May I?" he asked before his mouth made contact.

"Please," she managed.

He lowered her bodice. Cool air rushed over her bared breasts, and her nipples tightened. Further. Her nipples tightened *further*. They had already become taut peaks from the first moment she realized where his kisses were headed.

She gasped when his mouth closed around the tip of her breast. His tongue toyed with her nipple the way his tongue had played with hers during their kisses. Every lick ricocheted throughout her entire body, causing an unbearable ache to build between her legs.

As if sensing her need, he reached toward her skirts to pull up her hems.

He froze when his palm spanned the top of her stocking, just above her knee. "What's this?"

"Silk," she replied innocently.

She couldn't help but tease him. Of course he was not asking her to name the style of fabric. And what material it was! Madame Theroux had supplied several pairs of stockings in the softest, smoothest silk, each dyed a scandalous color. Today's were pink. Ever since her waltz with Titus, Matilda had donned a new pair every morning just in case there was a chance he might glimpse her undergarments and be tempted.

And *oh* was he tempted!

He tossed her hems up to her thighs without ceremony in his eagerness to feast his eyes on her silk-clad legs, with their garters made of Swiss lace threaded with sinful scarlet ribbons.

She hid a grin. "Does it please you?"

"Please me?" He smoothed his palms up her legs,

then ran a fingertip beneath the lacy flounce of her garter. "I wish I had five mouths so that I could kiss you everywhere at once."

"Try your best," she teased.

"Don't you worry. I will."

Rather than raise his lips back to her bosom, he allowed his hands to caress her breasts instead. As for his mouth, Titus lowered his face between her thighs, kissing the exposed skin above each garter, then slowly moving his way north, tossing aside her skirts with his teeth to expose more and more of her flesh, until—

Matilda's mouth fell open in surprise when his tongue touched the place she'd hoped he would caress with his fingers. Shockwaves rippled through her. This was infinitely better, and far more scandalous than pink silk stockings.

Her head lolled against the arm of the chaise longue at the onslaught of sensation. His fingers on her breasts and nipples, his mouth between her legs. In no time, the pressure that had been gathering since their first kiss built to a crescendo. Before she could warn him that she was dangling on the edge, her body exploded with pulsing waves of pleasure.

Only when the tremors ceased did he still his fingers and lift his head to press a kiss against her thigh. "We can stop here, if you like."

"Don't you dare." Her voice was raspy, every sated muscle limp. She reached for him anyway. "I want it all."

He fumbled for the fall of his trousers.

She shook her head. "In the nude, please. Both of us."

His face paled. "I—I can't."

"You can't disrobe without a valet? I am certain I can help you."

"No, it's not that. I can manage on my own. I always do. I've never let anyone see…"

She ran her hands over his fully clothed chest. "You think you'll frighten me away? Nonsense. There can be no doubt in your mind that I want you."

Indecision warred on his face, followed by firm resolve. "You first."

She twisted to expose the ribbon lacing her gown up her spine.

He untied the bow in seconds, lifting her gown and her shift together. They sailed up over her head to land in a heap somewhere behind the chaise.

"Now you." She reached for the buttons of his coat. "May I?"

He looked as though he were facing a firing squad, but he nodded grimly.

She unbuttoned the coat and pushed it off him, one shoulder at a time. The muslin sleeves of his white shirt billowed from his blue silk waistcoat. She unfastened that next, slipping the blue silk from his shoulders and onto the floor.

His oversized white shirt sagged down, the soft muslin brushing against her naked breasts and abdomen.

She started to raise the bottom hem. He stiffened, but did not stop her.

Every inch of exposed flesh revealed new scars. It was not just his face that had been permanently altered in the accident. His taut abdomen and wide chest also bore thick, puckered lines as if he had been lanced mercilessly with a sword.

Or dashed against the sharp rocks of a river, in the wreckage of a metal carriage.

"Oh, Titus," she murmured softly.

He glared at her. "I don't want your pity."

"You don't have it, you foolish man. Only you

could think the marks of your past continue to define you in the future." She tossed the shirt aside and spread her fingers against the warmth of his chest. "You're still the most beautiful gentleman I've ever seen."

He shook his head. "I'm—"

"*Perfect*," she said firmly, trailing her fingertips down to his waistband. "Now, wasn't there some- thing else you wanted to show me?"

He shucked his boots and his trousers as if there were a prize to be won for breaking the record for fastest disrobing.

Matilda's eyes widened at the sight of his shaft, but she could not ogle it for long. Soon it was hard and pulsing between her thighs, rubbing against the place where she was still wet and rapidly regaining that glorious sense of building pressure.

Titus's mouth devoured hers. Every muscle tensed in anticipation. "You're certain about this?"

She wrapped her legs about his hips. "Stop making me wait."

He wasted no more time.

She gasped as he entered her. A brief sting of pain followed quickly by mounting pleasure. She clasped her arms about him and held on tight. Her hips rose to meet his. He claimed her again and again with his mouth and body.

She was his. Utterly, irrevocably his. Ruined for all others. Bound to him for eternity. Nothing could diminish the earth-shattering connection they had forged.

Not even goodbye.

CHAPTER 29

The next morning, Matilda awoke alone, which was how she had succumbed to fitful sleep. After making love, Titus had cuddled her close until her eyes grew drowsy, then helped her to dress and find her way upstairs before too many household eyebrows could raise.

If Buttons suspected anything as she'd helped ready her mistress for bed, she refrained from saying a word. Nor was a single comment made in the morning, after Buttons had presumably had the opportunity to gossip with the other servants, if indeed there was any gossip to be had.

Matilda should be relieved. Her reputation wasn't ruined. No one had any idea.

It only made her want to do it all over again.

Titus, for his part, made no mention of the prior night either. When she entered the usual dining room, instead of greeting her with a kiss or even a secret smile, he simply offered to serve her breakfast. Very gentlemanly. Very *guardian*ly.

Not at all what Matilda wanted.

In fact, come to think of it—

"Happy birthday," he blurted out, as if they'd had

189

ERICA RIDLEY

the same thought at the same time. "You're not my ward anymore."

"What am I, then?" she asked softly.

"Miss Sour Lemon," he replied, willfully miscon-struing her question.

She tried to concentrate on her eggs and kippers.

He kept sneaking odd looks at her. Not in a sen-sual fashion, unless he was also feeling amorous to-ward the tall case clock in the corner. Titus seemed on edge. Every sound made him flinch.

Finally, she could stand it no more. "Are you all right?"

"I'm fine," he said quickly. Too quickly. "Are you finished with your breakfast?"

He hadn't touched his toast, as far as she could tell.

"I suppose I could be finished, if you're rushing me. Are we going somewhere?"

"*I'm* not," he said in obvious confusion.

Ah. Merely eager for her impending departure, then. She stabbed her eggs, then let her fork fall onto her plate. "I've no more appetite."

"Good." He launched himself to his feet and held out his elbow for her. "Allow me to escort you."

"Escort me where?" she asked in exasperation. "Upstairs to my valise?"

"No!" He looked lost for a second, then tugged her toward the corridor. "To the grand parlor."

"What's so grand about it?" she muttered. "It may be big enough to host a ball, but there's nothing in there but empty—"

Four dozen people sprang at her at once as she crossed the threshold.

"Surprise!" their voices shouted in unison.

Confetti swirled down from the chandelier.

"What... *is* this?" she asked in bewilderment.

"A party," Titus said with pride. "My very first. And with any luck, my last. It's for you."

"A party for me?" she repeated in wonder.

"A birthday party," he explained. "Or an independence day party, if you prefer. I wasn't certain if I should have everyone yell 'Happy birthday' or 'Happy majority' so we settled on simply 'Surprise'. *Was* it a surprise?"

"I'm still wrapping my head around it," she admitted.

No one had ever thrown a surprise anything for her before. The room was filled with smiling faces, all of whom belonged to people Matilda recognized. Lady Tabitha, grinning the widest. Aunt Stapleton, looking smug that her machinations had gone so swimmingly.

And every single gentleman Matilda had ever danced with.

She shot a suspicious look toward Titus. After last night—and her newfound independence—was he still somehow trying to matchmake her to...

No, that wasn't it at all. He was still glaring holes through every gentleman who dared to raise a glass of champagne in her honor, and visibly restrained himself from stepping between them whenever one of the men approached her to wish happy birthday in person.

This was exactly what he'd said it was: a party. For Matilda.

She made her way about the room, greeting each of the guests and accepting bites of cake and sips of champagne. For most of the revelers, the surprise was not Matilda's birthday, but that they had been invited to the Earl of Gilbourne's residence at all.

"Don't get used to it," she said with a laugh. "I'd

judge you have approximately one hour before he reaches his limit and sends you all home."

"What about you?" Lady Tabitha asked. "Rumor has it you're an heiress now. Will you be fishing for a husband in this buffet?"

"No," Matilda answered. "I'm not..." *interested in any of them?* A lie. She was madly in love with one of them.

The one standing in the shadowiest corner with his arms crossed and his face scowling like the devil.

"I dreamt of this moment," Matilda told her. "Of reaching my majority and being granted the freedom to have all the adventure I might desire."

"It sounds lovely," Lady Tabitha said with undisguised envy. "What will you do first with your independence?"

"Leave," she said quietly.

"Greece?" Lady Tabitha guessed. "Paris? Rome? America?"

Matilda shook her head.

Titus had intimated she could stay here in his home with him for as long as she liked, but Matilda had no wish to become a dirty secret. Not that their relationship, if the physical aspect were to continue, would stay secret for long.

She should soon be suspected a fallen woman. Her reputation, ruined. And hope of a future match, gone in a flash. Worth it? At first, she'd thought maybe it would be. Matilda did not *want* some other man. She wanted Titus.

But if he was unwilling to give his full self... She was not willing to live half a life. To never be fully accepted or chosen.

Better to leave now while she still had her pride.

"Rutland," she answered.

Lady Tabitha's forehead lined. "Rutland? What's that?"

"A country hamlet in the East Midlands. I've a small cottage there."

"You're going to live one hundred miles away?" Lady Tabitha said in surprise.

Her voice must have carried. Titus materialized at Matilda's side and turned her to face him.

His face was colorless. "You're leaving London?"

"I'm going home."

"But this *is*..." He swallowed. "I hoped you'd find lodgings nearby. I thought you'd... remain close. Lady Stapleton plans to stay in town for the next several months. I assumed you'd want..."

Matilda held his gaze. "Sometimes a clean break is the only way to heal."

If there was ever a moment to throw himself at her feet and beg her to stay, this was it.

He visibly collected himself instead. "Well, you can't rent a hackney to cover one hundred miles. Take one of my carriages."

"How will I return it to you?"

He shrugged. "Keep it."

"And the driver?" she asked.

"He'll remain on my payroll. Buttons, as well. She belongs with you now, for as long as you both please. I'll cover any associated costs."

"It seems you've thought of everything."

His jaw flexed. "Are you unhappy?"

Deeply. She smiled. "Thank you for the party, and the gifts. You are all that is considerate. I've left you a present as well."

He frowned. "Where? What is it?"

"It's a surprise," she said softly. "I guess this is the day for them."

CHAPTER 30

$\mathcal{B}$y noon, Titus finally had what he'd thought he wanted: his house back to normal again.

The guests were gone. His ward had just left. Every room they had ever been in together, now lay empty and silent.

Even before Matilda had gone, he'd felt the empty silence creeping in. As she'd climbed up into his carriage, the sharp sense of loss had excavated him, turning his insides out.

He'd wanted to stop her. To lay down before the horses if necessary. Better for the punishing hoofs and iron wheels to mince what was left of him, than to face a lifetime without Matilda.

But she deserved to be free. Even if it meant free of *him*.

Especially if it meant free of him.

Titus stalked from room to room, scowling at the noiseless interiors. The grand parlor, where he'd hosted his first and only party. The dining room, where he and Matilda had shared every meal. The library, where they had shared so much more. The chaise longue, where they had made love, just last night.

He stretched out on the chaise and tried to summon her warmth or her scent. It was useless. The maids had already come in to clean. They'd left everything spotless, just as he liked it. Not a speck of Matilda remained.

He'd fire the lot of them.

He covered his face with his hands, then curled sideways onto the chaise as though he were snuggling Matilda from behind. He wished he were. He'd cuddle her any way she would let him. But there was nothing in his arms but cold empty air. He no longer even had Oliver's old blanket, to try and wring a few more threads of comfort out of that.

With a growl of frustration, he dragged himself up from the chaise and stalked into his study. There was work to be done.

He didn't feel like doing any of it.

To the devil with Parliament. Someone else on his committees could write a speech for once. Titus would not be the star of the show today.

He trudged up the stairs, passing the housekeeper along the way.

She looked at him with pity.

Titus despised being the recipient of pity. And he hated worse that Mrs. Harris was right: Titus was absolutely a messy, miserable wreck. He couldn't even muster up the will to threaten to sack her for her unsolicited compassion.

At the top of the stairs, he started to head to his bedchamber and return to his bed, from which he might not emerge for decades. But at the last second, he turned in the opposite direction, and entered the room that had been Matilda's guest chamber instead.

A parcel sat atop the neatly made bed.

He frowned and edged forward. A folded square was tucked beneath the twine.

It read:

TITUS

in clean, bold print.
Underneath was scrawled:

For Gilly-Gil-Gil.

Titus let out a soft snort. How had she known he would miss her so viscerally, he would come in here hoping for the tiniest remnant of their connection?

He sat down on the edge of the bed and pulled the parcel into his lap. Titus set the note aside. He would read that last. He was dying to know what sort of gift she thought a man like him most longed for.

The parcel felt soft and light and lumpy. As if it perhaps contained the garters and silk stockings she had worn the night before.

He untied the knot, slid the twine aside, and unwrapped the parcel. Not garters after all.

Oliver's blanket.

Matilda had sewn it back together.

He hugged it to his chest, burying his face in its familiar softness. It had lost the scent of Oliver long ago, but now smelled faintly of Matilda.

That wasn't the only change. The new seams, like Titus's old scars, were obvious. But Oliver's blanket was whole again. Whole and home, and back in Titus's arms. He tried not to sob.

When he could bear to release the blanket, he reached for the note. It read:

Nothing can ever return exactly as it was,
but rifts can often be mended.

HE STARED down at the scarred, beloved blanket in his hands, then rose to his feet with determination.

She was right. He had wasted enough of his life by centering his focus on the things he had lost, never appreciating the new things he had found—until he'd lost them, as well.

Titus didn't want to waste any more of however much life he had left. He wanted to spend every minute that remained with the woman he loved.

If she would have him.

CHAPTER 31

*B*uttons was beside herself to be trundling along in the earl's grandest carriage. She practically hung out of the window to gape at all the sights—or to ensure all of the passers-by glimpsed a mere lady's maid, traveling face-forward in an elegant coach-and-four with the Earl of Gilbourne's unmistakable coat of arms painted on the side.

Matilda was less enthusiastic.

The drive would take fourteen long hours *if* they were lucky. The further the carriage got from London, the worse the roads would become. By the time they reached the East Midlands, there would be sections with ruts big enough to bathe in.

Not that any of that was what was bothering her.

There had been a brief moment when Titus had handed her into the carriage, when she'd thought, just for a second, that maybe he might...

But he hadn't. Of course he hadn't. He'd *told* her he wouldn't. The first thing he'd said to her once he'd learned she was his ward was that he couldn't wait for the day she would leave. Last night, when she was naked in his arms, nothing had changed.

Matilda could dress up as a fine lady, could memorize every note she jotted down in her notebook, but when it was time to stay or to leave…

She wasn't good enough for him.

"Um… Miss?" said Buttons.

"I told you," Matilda said tiredly. "I don't care what's outside the window. Wake me up when we reach Rutland."

But no matter how tight she closed her eyes, she could not block the memory of Titus's face. How he'd looked, in the throes of passion. How everyone else had looked, that time he'd smiled at her in front of all and sundry on the dance floor. The soft heat of his kisses all over her body.

"Miss," fretted Buttons. "I really think you ought to see—"

"Oh, for God's sake, what is it? Another pretty church?" Matilda leaned forward and swung her annoyed gaze outside the window.

There, drawing alongside the carriage, was a horseman.

Not just any horseman. *Titus*. Riding bareback, dressed all in black, save for a familiar square white blanket tied about his neck like a cape, fluttering behind him in the wind as he spurred his horse faster.

Matilda rapped the driver's panel frantically, then called through the hole, "Stop the horses!"

The coachman halted the horses at once.

Matilda flung open the door. She needn't step down from the carriage to be at eye level with Titus. Astride a tall stallion, he looked magnificent. And a little bit ridiculous. The cape was a wonderful, absurdist touch, and secured in place with what looked like a diamond pin.

"Stand and deliver?" she asked archly.

"Only if you're offering your heart," he replied, then took a deep breath. "You already have mine."

"Other carriages are stopping," Buttons whispered. "People are gawking."

Matilda batted her back toward the interior. "*Shh.* I don't want to miss this."

"When I first met you," Titus said, "I thought being orphaned was the only thing we had in common. It quickly became clear our wounds had affected us in opposite ways. I shut down and closed off, whilst you did your best to make as many connections as possible." His eyes held hers. "In the end, perhaps I just needed one. The right one."

Her heart fluttered.

He carefully unfastened the stitched-together white cape from about his shoulders and held it up. "Thank you for returning my brother's blanket. I don't know why you had it in the first place—"

"Don't you dare sack Augustin."

"I will not sack Augustin. I will double Augustin's wages. He entrusted you with my broken pieces, and you put me back together. I hadn't wanted to let go of the blanket because I wanted to rewrite that moment. To let Oliver find comfort wherever he could. Allow my father to keep his eyes on the road. The horses, safe. My family, alive. But the moment I was trying to hold onto is long gone."

She swallowed hard.

He tied the cape back onto his neck. "All along, the moments I *should* have been trying to hold onto were the ones I shared with you. I can't get back the loved ones I lost. But I could make a bloody effort not to lose another one."

She held her breath. Was he saying...

He continued, "I thought the best way to never again lose someone I love, was by not allowing anyone in to begin with. If I walled off my heart, I wouldn't care when others inevitably left me. But you slipped inside and left me defenseless. I care so deeply, no walls can contain my heart. It no longer belongs to me. It belongs to you."

Buttons was right. They were attracting an audience. More passers-by were peering at them from the street and from their carriages than were actually passing on by.

Matilda didn't care. She could not have moved a muscle if she'd tried.

"This *is* a marriage proposal, by the way," Titus added with a sheepish smile. "The one I should have given you last night. Or the night before. Or the night before that. The only acceptable time frame to spend with you is forever. I've known it since the labyrinth. And suspected it since the moment I glimpsed you behind that potted plant."

Someone let out a cheer, and was summarily shushed by the growing crowd.

"I want to be the one who brings you candied lemon peels," he said softly. "I want to be the knight who saves you from spiders. I want to be whatever it is that you need, now and always. You've seen the worst of me. Please let me give you the best of me."

Buttons edged forward to stage-whisper, "Milord, *ask the actual question.*"

Titus cleared his throat. "Miss Matilda 'Candied Orange Peel' Dodd, would you please do me the honor—"

"Yes!" she blurted out, and launched herself into his arms.

Titus caught her. As soon as she was safe, the stallion dashed forward, forging a path through the crowd and galloping off in a random direction.

Matilda clung to Titus's neck. The cape flapped behind them. He held on tight. She did the same. "Where is your horse taking us?"

"I have no idea." He peppered her face with kisses. "Do you mind?"

She shook her head and kissed him. "The destination doesn't matter, as long as we're together."

It was all part of the adventure.

EPILOGUE

Rutland, England
Three months later

The Earl of Gilbourne's knees dug into the soft earth behind a pretty—if minuscule—cottage that could fit inside of his parlor, if he moved a few chairs. Luckily they were only here for a brief visit to check on Matilda's ancestral home.

His countess was also down on her hands and knees. Unfortunately, she was not doing anything Titus would have preferred her to do whilst in that position.

Matilda brought a smile to his face anyway. She always did. And maybe one day soon, their family would grow even bigger.

"Have we finished yet?" he asked for the third time in a row.

She glared at him. "You'll know when we've finished, because all the weeds will be gone from the garden."

"You know we could hire someone to do this. Better yet, I could hire someone to walk to a market where somebody else has *already* done all of this, and all he or she need do is to bring back a basket of vegetables."

"We're having fun," his countess said firmly.

He plucked a stray leaf from her hair. "Do you know what else is fun?"

Matilda's cheeks flushed pink. "We did that already this morning."

"Is there a limit I'm unaware of?"

"You *might* get another opportunity…" She ran a finger down his chest. "…if you help me finish plucking out these weeds."

Titus launched himself into the task with verve, digging into the soil and tossing weeds over his shoulder like the world's smallest tempest.

Which might also be how the stray leaf had found its way into his wife's hair to begin with.

"All right, all right," she said, laughing. "If you 'help' much more, you'll destroy the entire garden."

"I'll buy you a new one," he promised. "We're really done?"

"For now," she warned him. "And only if you entertain me properly."

He leapt to his feet and scooped her into his arms. "I live to entertain you."

"A jester, are you?"

"A fool in love," Titus agreed. He kissed the tip of her nose and swung her toward the cottage.

She wrapped her arms about his neck and kissed his cheeks. "I love you, Gilly-bear."

"I love you more, Mattie-Mat-Mat," he growled as he elbowed his way into the house. "My wife. My countess. My love."

The door banged behind them, followed soon by the squeak of a mattress.

They never did return to the garden.

THANK YOU

AND SNEAK PEEKS

THANK YOU FOR READING

Love talking books with fellow readers?

Join the *Historical Romance Book Club* for prizes, books, and live chats with your favorite romance authors:

Facebook.com/groups/HistRomBookClub

Check out the **Patreon** for bonus content, sneak peeks, advance review copies and more:

https://www.patreon.com/EricaRidleyFans

And don't miss the **official website**:

www.EricaRidley.com/books

ABOUT THE AUTHOR

Erica Ridley is a *New York Times* and *USA Today* best-selling author of witty, feel-good historical romance novels, including THE DUKE HEIST, featuring the Wild Wynchesters. Why seduce a duke the normal way, when you can accidentally kidnap one in an elaborately planned heist?

In the *12 Dukes of Christmas* series, enjoy witty, heartwarming Regency romps nestled in a picturesque snow-covered village. After all, nothing heats up a winter night quite like finding oneself in the arms of a duke!

Two popular series, the *Dukes of War* and *Rogues to Riches*, feature roguish peers and dashing war heroes who find love amongst the splendor and madness of Regency England.

When not reading or writing romances, Erica can be found eating couscous in Morocco, zip-lining through rainforests in Central America, or getting hopelessly lost in the middle of Budapest.

~

Let's be friends! Find Erica on:
www.EricaRidley.com